Bewitched, Body and Soul

Miss Elizabeth Bennet

P O Dixon

Bewitched, Body and Soul: Miss Elizabeth Bennet

ISBN-13: 978-1475275773
ISBN-10: 1475275773

Dedicated with love to my beautiful daughter, Elizabeth.

Acknowledgments

The highest praise goes to Miss Jane Austen for her timeless works and to the JAFF community for its curiosity in asking, "What if?"

I offer heartfelt thanks to Gayle, Stephanie, and Robin for all their support throughout this effort. Their patience and their advice have made all the difference, and I am eternally grateful.

Contents

"Well, my comfort is, I am sure Jane will die of a broken heart, and then he will be sorry for what he has done."

Jane Austen, *Pride and Prejudice*

Chapter 1

"Mind you, my dear, a girl likes to be crossed in love a little now and then. It is something to think of and gives her a sort of distinction amongst her companions," Mr. Bennet teased as he fiddled with his gold pocket-watch. The middle-aged, silver-haired patriarch was far less inclined to fret over his eldest daughter's sufferings as vigorously as did the women of Longbourn Village. For goodness sake, they were some of the silliest creatures in all of England! This latest calamity—marked by the lack of spirit shown by his first-born daughter Jane, the refusal on her part to take her meals with the family, and the general disregard of all that once mattered to her—had gone on long enough.

"I dare say Jane is more than a little crossed," said Mrs. Bennet, her annoyance obvious. "Why, the way Mr. Bingley and his party fled Netherfield Park on the heels of what I was sure would be a proposal of marriage to the poor girl, has rendered her a laughing stock in the neighbourhood.

"I can imagine their jeers. 'There goes poor Miss Bennet, with all her beauty, yet abandoned ... practically left waiting at the altar for Mr. Bingley.'

"Oh, how shall she show her face again? I am afraid the dear girl is destined to a life of spinsterhood ... despite my good efforts to find a husband for her."

Mr. Bennet rubbed his brow. How nonsensical. With such a mother, it was no wonder his daughters were such frivolous creatures. He opened his mouth to make light of her sentiments as regarded the neighbours' gossip when the door opened.

If twenty-odd years of marriage had taught him anything, it was to welcome the sight of his second eldest, and by far, his favourite daughter whenever his wife went on in that way. Mr. Bennet silently applauded Elizabeth's timely arrival.

"A life of spinsterhood, Mama? Which of your five unfortunate daughters do you speak of now?"

"I might as well be speaking of any of you, save Kitty and my Lydia. However, I speak at this moment of Jane. I dare say she did little, if anything, to encourage Mr. Bingley. The way he looked at her, I am sure it would not have taken much for him to propose marriage. This wretched situation brings to mind a similar event several years back when that delightful young man from town showed a keen interest in her. As I recall, he wrote her some lovely poetry—" Her voice trailed off as her face echoed a look of nostalgia.

"Surely, Mama, you cannot blame Jane for Mr. Bingley's lack of consideration. Jane loves him. I am sure of it. One needed only to spend time with her in his company to attest to that fact. Mr. Bingley is a fool not to perceive her true worth."

"A fool he may be, but it is hardly a consolation. Better a fool for a son-in-law, than no son-in-law at all." Mrs. Bennet narrowed her eyes on her daughter. "And do not think for one moment that your rejection of Mr. Collins's hand reflects kindly upon you, Miss Lizzy."

"Mrs. Bennet, I commend my Lizzy for rejecting Mr. Collins."

"Indeed. The two of you can take great comfort in going against my adamant wish that Lizzy should accept Mr. Collins. At the least, I might have seen one of my daughters settled by now. Alas, Lizzy, your *so-called* friend, Charlotte Lucas, put an end to that hope."

"Mama, you know I bear Charlotte no ill-will for having accepted Mr. Collins's offer of marriage. Charlotte is practical. She merely acted in the best interests of her family."

"The best interests of *her* family you say. What of your own family? Are the Lucases more worthy than our family of the security afforded by a daughter well-settled, married to the heir of Longbourn, no less, owing to that ridiculous entail?"

"My dear Mrs. Bennet, you shall not place the liability of our family's fate at Lizzy's feet."

"I should say not, Mr. Bennet. I am afraid the burden of finding suitable husbands for our daughters rests upon my shoulders alone. To have suffered the loss of not one but two future sons-in-law, I know not how I shall recover from such a misfortune." The aggrieved mistress of the manor, whose countenance hinted of her former good looks, gathered her mending and stood to quit the room. "Take heed, Miss Lizzy, for you shall expect no help from me in securing another gentleman as your future husband. You are quite on your own in that regard.

"I suggest you take my brother and sister up on their invitation to stay with them in town in Jane's stead. Then you might stand a decent chance. I only wish my Lydia or even Kitty had such opportunity."

ജരുജരു

Her dearest sister sat in the window seat with one hand pressed against the windowpane, absent-minded of the seeping chill of the January air. In the other hand, she clutched the post she had received weeks ago from Miss Caroline Bingley, the sister of her lost lover.

Surely, she has committed every word to memory by now. How many weeks more might she carry on this way? Elizabeth had done her best to persuade her favourite sister that there had been a misunderstanding. Mr. Bingley loved her. Somehow, his pernicious sister had managed to poison his mind against Jane.

"Jane, you must resist this urge to surrender yourself to the gloom and despair wrought by the constant perusal of Miss Bingley's letter. The lies she expounded therein are not rendered as truth by subsequent reading, I assure you."

"Lizzy, I do not believe Miss Bingley lied. Without question, Mr. Bingley would prefer Miss Darcy to a penniless gentleman's daughter. Why would he not be eager to return to town ... to her?"

"Penniless? I dare say I have never heard you speak ill of our father's fortune, or lack thereof. This smacks of bitterness. To give in to bitterness is to allow the likes of Miss Bingley to prevail." She walked to her sister, sat in the window seat next to her, and reached for her hand.

"Jane, Mr. Bingley conducted himself exactly as would a man in love whenever he was with you. Miss Bingley is the one who desires an alliance between her brother and Miss Darcy. She observed how he adored you. You are a threat to her grand plan for an alliance between the Bingleys and the Darcys. She did everything in her power to separate you two."

Answering such sentiments with silence, Jane refused her sister's proffered hand.

"I remember how you were dead set against returning to town with our Uncle and Aunt Gardiner after Christmas for a chance to meet Mr. Bingley and undo the damage caused by his sister. I pray you have changed your mind." Elizabeth stroked her sister's forearm. "Do you not believe it is worth fighting for the man you love?"

Jane kept her angelic blue eyes, eyes laden with despair, trained out of the window, staring aimlessly. She clutched her arms in front of her chest.

"Jane," Elizabeth placed her hand on her sister's shoulder, "come away from the window, dearest. Let us sit by the fire and decide what we might do to right this wrong. It pains me when you carry on so."

Jane shrank from Elizabeth's touch. "Lizzy, please, leave it be! I refuse to chase after a man who subjected me to such ridicule and pain. I am afraid you are mistaken. He does not care for me. How could he? He knows what he has done. Even if what you say is true, that his mind has been poisoned against me, if he should one day realise it and decide he indeed loves me, he knows where I am. He knows where to find me."

"Jane—"

Jane placed her hands on her hips. Releasing an exasperated sigh, she raised her voice. "Hush, Lizzy, I beg of you. If you and I are to remain as the dearest of sisters, you must speak of this no more. I loved Mr. Bingley, and I love him until this day. I fear I may never love again, because I am sure I will never forget him. For now, it is all I can do to bear my mother's disappointment, much less endure our neighbours' scorn. I dare not show my face in Meryton. I certainly shall not travel to London."

Her sister returned her listless gaze to the stillness outside her window. "I wish only to be left alone."

Elizabeth honoured Jane's request and stood to leave the room. She turned to study her sister before opening the door and sighed. Pulling the door closed, Elizabeth rested her head against it. *This must not go on. I feel as though I no longer recognise my sister.*

5

Her eyebrow arched, she twisted her lower lip. *If this is what it is like to be in love, may I never have the pleasure. Jane continues to walk around, clutching that venomous letter from Caroline Bingley. And to what end? She is making herself ridiculous.* The guilt Elizabeth felt with that pronouncement caused her to consider that perhaps she was too hard on Jane. Her closest friend, Charlotte, had warned that Mr. Bingley might abandon his hopes if Jane did not do anything to encourage his tender regard. Jane's character would never have allowed such a display of her true feelings.

Perhaps I might take my Aunt and Uncle Gardiner up on their invitation to stay with them in town. I could surely benefit from a reprieve from Mama's near constant chastisement on my refusal of Mr. Collins. Then, I might also find a way to uncover the cause of this misunderstanding with Mr. Bingley.

Elizabeth collected herself and hurried down the stairs. She needed a long walk to sort things out. She donned her bonnet and cloak and set off on her favourite path. The farther she walked, the deeper the notion of venturing to town took root. So, too, did a measure of doubt creep into her thoughts.

Her brow furrowed, she pursed her lips. *What if I am wrong? What if I should learn that Mr. Bingley truly does not care for Jane?* Elizabeth balked at the notion. She prided herself on being much too astute a studier of people not to recognise a man in love when she saw one.

Undoubtedly, he cares. I am never mistaken about these things.

ಬಚಿಚಿಬ

"Mary, I am depending upon you to watch over Jane. Do what you must in trying to divert her, to keep her spirits up. Do not allow her to wallow in grief and misery over the prospect of never again seeing Mr. Bingley." Elizabeth busied herself with packing her things whilst Mary looked on.

Her next eldest sister's face teemed with scepticism, no

doubt over the judiciousness of Elizabeth's scheme. She opened her mouth to say something, but no words spouted forth.

Quite determined, Elizabeth pretended not to notice. "I
shall also look forward to hearing from you of what is happening here at Longbourn during my absence."

Mary cleared her throat. "Lizzy, I applaud your gener-
osity and selflessness as regards our sister's well-being, but I
am afraid I do not approve of your tactics. Must I remind you
of the results the last time you tossed propriety to the wind by
traipsing about the countryside in your desire to attend Jane
after she fell ill at Netherfield Park, casting all semblance of
decorum aside? Although I had no luck in persuading you
against your purposes then, I believe I owe it to my own sense
of modesty to try again to compel you to consider the folly of
your plan.

"In my opinion, the course you are set upon is guided
less by reason and prudence than by a desire to manipulate
events best left to others."

Elizabeth halted her packing and sat on the bed beside
her sister. "Mary, what harm could come as a result of my
plans? If I am to be in town anyway, as I already have an acquaintance with Miss Bingley, surely I risk nothing in calling
on her. Just imagine how happy Jane will be once this misunderstanding is resolved. However, you must not say a word
of my plans to anyone. This must be our secret, just in case
things do not go as intended; there is no need to increase
Jane's hopes."

"Lizzy, I long for the recovery of Jane's spirits as much
as you, but surely your absence will cause her even greater disappointment. She loves you. What is more, she depends upon
you."

"You are correct. I love her, and you know I would do
anything in the world to see her happy, which is why I must
do everything in my power to reunite her with the man she

loves."

"And if, indeed, Mr. Bingley's actions speak to his true intentions, then what?"

"Oh, Mary, Mr. Bingley loves Jane. However, on the chance that he does not, it is even more imperative to keep my undertaking a secret. This way, no one shall be disappointed … no one except me."

"My sentiments exactly—disappointed and perhaps embarrassed. Take care that you do not make a spectacle of yourself." Mary adjusted her glasses. "I need not remind you how tender a thing is a woman's reputation—how once lost, is nearly impossible to recover."

Elizabeth had given greater consideration to Mary's words than she had allowed. Alone in her room, she completed her packing and sat on the bed beside her luggage. She knew what she was about. She planned to find out for herself if there was an attachment between Mr. Bingley and Miss Darcy, or if this was a ruse on Miss Bingley's part.

If it is indeed true, if there is an attachment, no one will be disappointed any more than already, and the only risk of harm is the damage to my ego.

Elizabeth stood and took a final look around the room. She decided it was worth the risk. She must speak to Mr. Bingley directly. Somehow, even if it meant calling on her least favourite person in the world, she planned to make her presence in town known and find a way to be in Mr. Bingley's company.

Jane needs me. I shall not let her down.

Chapter 2

Darcy stretched his arms over his head, and then gripped his broad shoulder and worked out his tightened muscles. He questioned the wisdom of arriving in town to his London home earlier than scheduled. Despite his frequent and lengthy absences, he had expected the presence of more staff. He had notified his butler of his plans to return the following week. Perhaps that had been the problem. However, he was there now, and much needed to be done to make the place habitable for the evening. There would be time enough to address his London household staffing shortfalls later. Determined, Darcy and his valet made do by taking up the task of preparing the fires and lighting the rooms.

He had spent the past few weeks at the country estate of his friend, Lord Trevor Helmsley, the Earl of Latham. Darcy reflected upon the purpose of his friend's invitation to spend time at his home before the start of the Season, or rather the irony. Imagine his luck. Two of his closest friends both had single sisters, and both young ladies had set their sights upon marriage—to him. There the similarity ended. The two young ladies were as different as night and day. One, Lady Gwendolen, was an accomplished young woman whose aristocratic roots marked her entire being, and whose kindness outshone her beauty and grace. The other, Caroline, was a ridiculous social climber whose sole redeeming quality was her relationship to Charles Bingley.

The manner in which Darcy had gone out of his way in pretending not to notice Lady Gwendolen over the past weeks had not ranked amongst his finest moments. The last thing he wanted was to encourage her expectations. The seven years since he had first met her had done much in transforming her from the shy girl, who scarcely uttered a word in his presence, to the beautiful, blossoming young woman she had become. The upcoming Season would be her third. Darcy wondered why no man had requested her hand in marriage.

On the other hand, perhaps someone has. Indeed, she is holding out for someone. Holding out for me ... her brother insinuated as much. What a shame to give up any immediate chances for happiness on the hope of something that might never be.

Darcy shook his head, walked to his liquor cabinet, and prepared himself a drink. He savoured the smooth drink as it slid down his throat.

By contrast, as regards Caroline, even with her twenty thousand pounds, I would be surprised if anyone has requested her hand in marriage. She would be wise to accept any offer she gets rather than waste her time fawning over me.

The vicious manner in which she had disparaged the Bennet women in Hertfordshire, saying they would be hard-pressed to find suitable husbands, was deplorable.

Moreover, think how I agreed with her, dare say even encouraged her, in a foolish attempt to disguise my inexplicable attraction to Elizabeth.

Miss Elizabeth Bennet. A woman who walked three miles to a neighbouring estate, arriving unescorted and with her hem six inches deep in mud. *She is unlike any other woman of my ac-*

quaintance, to say the least. I do not imagine Caroline doing such a thing. Lady Gwendolen, however ... she might. He called to mind accounts from his friend, Lord Latham, of how his young sister tossed such formalities as always being in the company of an escort aside, when in the country. Darcy also recalled saying several times how he would not wish for his own sister to behave so.

His sister, Georgiana, had suffered many trials of late. He had allowed her to travel to Ramsgate with a Mrs. Younge, her former companion. There, she had been followed and nearly ruined by his nemesis, George Wickham. He was thankful that she had come to grips with what had happened in Ramsgate and had accepted his account that George Wickham truly did not love her, but had tried to persuade her to marry him as a means of getting her fortune of thirty thousand pounds. His motive—revenge.

What a hard lesson for a young girl of fifteen to learn. Darcy took some comfort in his belief that his sister had got over the worst of it.

Again, his mind wandered to his friends Lord Latham and Bingley, and their sisters, neither of whom would behave so recklessly. However, they were older than Georgiana, and by virtue of their ages, wiser.

Darcy ran his fingers through his hair. *Why am I thinking of those two, neither of whom is Elizabeth? Then again, why would I even think of her?*

Darcy threw back his drink in one swig. *Irony indeed.* He had spent the best part of the past few months in the company of two women who made no secret of their desire to bear his name. *One, who is everything that is good; the other, who is everything of bad, and neither of whom is the woman I dream of whenever I close my eyes; neither is the one woman who threatened to capture my heart, had I remained in Hertfordshire. What a shame she is wholly unsuitable, owing to her low connections.*

Fortunately, he had saved himself—from himself. Whilst

dancing with her during the Netherfield ball, it took everything he could muster not to take her in his arms, and with a brush of his lips against hers, silence her words in defence of that scoundrel George Wickham. Of course, such an outrageous act would have branded him an even worse scoundrel. On the other hand, she would be mistress of Pemberley by now.

One thing he considered—the past weeks had taught him that it would take more than time and distance to release him from the spell of the beguiling country miss who managed to captivate him with a nod of her head, a witty turn of phrase, and a teasing smile. Try as he might, he could not stop thinking of her. Every morning upon waking, he wondered how she would spend her day. Every night before sleeping, his heart ached from having suffered another day apart from her.

Darcy took a seat by the fireplace, rested his head in his hands, and closed his eyes. Captivating looks in the stunning, dark eyes of an enchanting woman with a light, pleasing figure flooded his mind. How he missed her, missed challenging her, trading wits with her, and simply admiring her. It would not do. He need never see her again. The sooner he reconciled his heart and mind to that fact, the better.

The pounding of the doorknocker had sounded twice before Darcy remembered he would have to answer it. He might have ignored it but for his plans to dine with his friend, Charles Bingley, that evening. Darcy's valet had placed the knocker on the door at his request on the chance that Bingley might come around to his townhouse instead of meeting him at the club.

He and Bingley had spent little time in company since taking their leave of Hertfordshire. Bingley's barely legible letters offered no hints of his state of mind regarding Miss Jane Bennet, Elizabeth's eldest sister. He prayed he would not have to spend the entire evening listening to his friend lament his long-lost angel.

Darcy threw open the heavy door. "I dare say ..." His words trailed off. Astonished, he beheld a most alluring spectacle, stilling his words, nearly disquieting his heart.

She stared in wide-eyed expression rendered even lovelier by the gasp escaping her parted lips.

Chapter 3

S he expected to see his butler—dour, stone-faced, menacingly clad in black, and challenging the audacity of an unescorted young gentlewoman calling on an unmarried gentleman. So much for the speech that she had rehearsed on the way over, in hopes that it would speed her into Mr. Darcy's company without raising eyebrows.

Elizabeth summoned her courage, silenced her pounding heart, and smiled. Certainly, he must be surprised in seeing her. Decided incivility had marked their last meeting.

"Miss Elizabeth Bennet—" His voice sounded more piqued than astonished.

Why would it not? He is a wealthy single man who never looked at me for any reason, except to find fault. He barely tolerated my company before, yet here I stand on his doorstep, uninvited and unannounced.

"Mr. Darcy, I pray you do not find this an imposition. I have come here owing to a matter of some importance that I wish to discuss with you."

One hand placed on his hip, he gripped the heavy door

with the other, thus giving Elizabeth pause.

What was I thinking in coming here? "If this is not a good time, I can call again ... when it is convenient."

The cold, misty shower she had hoped would have passed by now took a nasty turn. Heavy rain poured down in sheets, sopping everything in its path. Elizabeth pulled her cloak tighter. The hood, weighed down by the rainwater, clung to her face. She imagined she appeared as a pitiable wet wretch.

Darcy glanced over his shoulder. Then, as his apprehensive expression eased, so did his grip. Though Elizabeth would have preferred a warm reception in place of his earlier put out scowl, his befuddled mien would have to suffice. Elizabeth covered her nose before trying unsuccessfully to prevent a sneeze from escaping. Another followed.

"Pardon me, Miss Elizabeth. Please, come inside. I cannot allow you to remain outside in such a deluge, and I cannot send you away. I do not see your carriage."

Elizabeth entered the grand foyer. She lowered the hood of her cloak to rest upon her shoulders.

"May I take your coat?" Elizabeth silently accommodated his request. "I am afraid you will find me ill-prepared to receive you properly, Miss Elizabeth. I returned to town only hours ago, days ahead of schedule. It seems my butler and staff are scattered about London attending ailing relatives and what not, I suppose, in view of my unannounced arrival," Darcy said. His voice rang with a hint of frustration.

Darcy looked about for a place to lay her cloak to rest whilst she remained speechless. Elizabeth could not open her mouth as she considered what had just happened. Mr. Darcy had answered his own door! No butler, no doorman, instead she found a rich gentleman performing a mere servant's task.

"Join me in my study."

The two walked the length of the foyer in silence. Rich smells of polished wood, and the warm glow of brass candelabras gave the place a feeling of home, quieting her anxiety even as she questioned her scheme. Darcy pushed the door open and stood aside to allow her to pass.

"Please have a seat." He gestured toward the chairs in front of his desk as he closed the door. Elizabeth did as told, and Darcy soon joined her. Rather than take a seat in the large leather chair behind the huge mahogany desk, Darcy sat in one of the armchairs about a foot away from Elizabeth. He rearranged his chair enough to face her.

She had expected the formal, reserved Mr. Darcy of whom she had learned to think poorly in Hertfordshire, and thus was astounded. He did not even wear a jacket. His shirt hung from his trousers, and his cuffs were undone. His dishabille was a stark contrast to his stately study. Except for a blanket, casually strewn upon his finely upholstered settee, the room was immaculate.

"Now, you say you came here because you suppose I might be of some service to you?"

"Indeed. Mr. Darcy—"

Darcy beckoned her silence by the haughty lifting of his chin. "I trust you did not walk here from Hertfordshire ... unescorted."

"No, I did not walk from Hertfordshire. I am staying in Cheapside with my Uncle and Aunt Gardiner." His ill-disguised grimace came as no surprise to Elizabeth. Whilst in Hertfordshire, he had made no attempt whatsoever to hide his disdain for everyone whom he deemed beneath him, which turned out to be everyone he met. She had no reason to suppose he might view her relatives from Cheapside any differently.

"Yet, you are unescorted."

"Mr. Darcy, you know as well as anyone of my propensity to come and go as I please. When have you known me to be accompanied by a maid when venturing about?"

"Do I need to remind you that you are not in Meryton?

What passes as appropriate behaviour there will be frowned upon amongst London's Society."

"I do not require a lecture from you on etiquette, at least not now. At the risk of exposing myself to Society's disdain, I came to you because you are Mr. Bingley's closest friend. My request is one which can be made only in person."

"Excuse me, Miss Elizabeth. Pray how did you know where to find me?"

"I came here by coach ... hackney."

"That does not explain how you were able to arrive on my doorstep."

"I asked my driver to make enquiries until we came upon your address. Finding you was easier than I thought it would be." Elizabeth raised her eyebrow. "I trust that does not harm your sensibilities."

Darcy shrugged. "I am in my home. Concern for *my* sensibilities is not the point."

"I trust you and I are sufficiently acquainted that I should not fear for my safety."

"That depends upon what you mean by safety. I believe it is incumbent upon me to inform you that you and I are the sole occupants of this house. Except for my valet who is out on errands, other members of the household staff are not expected until tomorrow."

Startled. *Only the two of us?* Elizabeth's heart beat as rapidly as the pounding of Mary's fingers when she practised her scales. She had hoped his young sister would be there, at the least, to lend some air of decorum to her visit. She removed the handkerchief from her sleeve. A muffled sneeze nearly escaped. She felt a slight chill creep over her body.

"Are you comfortable?"

"Yes—no," Elizabeth cradled her arms. Her body trembled. "I find it a bit nippy."

The warmth of the fire had not loosened the cold's grip

on the room. "Pardon me. Let us move by the fireplace." Darcy stood and led the way. "May I offer you a drink?"

"Please do not go to any trouble on my behalf."

Darcy walked over to the liquor cabinet to pour himself another drink. He also poured one for Elizabeth and returned to her side. He handed her the snifter of brandy. "I suffered no trouble."

With reluctance, Elizabeth accepted the proffered drink. What made him think she imbibed liquor? Did he mean to challenge her? She raised the glass to her lips and sipped the slightest of sips. Darcy sat in the seat opposite her and enjoyed a larger swallow.

Elizabeth set her drink aside and smoothed her skirt. His intent gaze was unsettling. She had never been as nervous in his company. She supposed she had long since grown immune to his impenetrable stare. Being in his home, alone with him before a comfortable fire, imbibing brandy, was not something she had planned. Unlike their meetings in Hertfordshire where their time in company at Netherfield Park was spent sparring, her matching his verbal challenges with witty repartee always rendering her the victor, he now clearly held the advantage.

"Your family ... I trust everyone is well, Miss Elizabeth?"

"Everybody is the same as when you departed, Mr. Darcy. Everybody, that is to say, save my sister Jane."

"Miss Bennet? Please continue."

"I fear there has been a grave misunderstanding on Mr. Bingley's part as regards Jane's sentiments. She loves him. The manner in which he took such precipitous leave of Netherfield Park destroyed her spirit. I fear she is in danger of its threatening her health."

"I dare say one does not suffer, physically, any ill-effects from disappointed hopes."

"Why should she suffer at all? She loves him. He loves her. I am convinced of their mutual affection; else, I would not have come here to correct an injustice."

Darcy shrugged. "Why did you come to me? You might have gone straight to Bingley with your *account*."

"Actually, Mr. Darcy, I did go directly to Mr. Bingley. At least, I attempted to. I just left there, in fact. His sister, Miss Bingley, received me. She wasted little time in apologising to me in Jane's stead, saying that her brother had thought better of his behaviour in Hertfordshire and deeply regretted raising Jane's hopes.

"When I told her that I would rather hear an explanation for his behaviour from him, she said he was away in the North, visiting family. I rather doubt her account and that is why I am here. Mr. Darcy, at the risk to my own reputation, I appeal to you, as Mr. Bingley's closest friend to intercede with him on my behalf."

Darcy frowned. "You might have come right out and said this upfront. What do you expect of me?"

"If what Miss Bingley says is true, that he is visiting family in the North, I appeal to you to write to him, telling him of Jane's sentiments."

"That will not be necessary. Bingley is in town."

"Then I would ask that you speak to him on my behalf. Tell him there has been a terrible misunderstanding as regards my sister's sentiments towards him, that his own sister has misled him. I dare say Miss Bingley will do everything in her power to keep me from seeing him in his home. He will surely believe you if you tell him of his sister's deception. Besides, he may take offence in hearing all this from me. However, your being his closest friend, having the information come from you will lend credence to my assertions."

Darcy closed his eyes and moaned. Elizabeth surmised with his groan that he had ignored her argument. "If nothing else, will you tell him that I am in town and that I wish to see him?"

"I fear you have come here for naught, Miss Elizabeth. I do not intend to intervene on any family's behalf regardless of their needs in matters of marriage. The choice of a bride must be beneficial to both parties."

"How can you refuse me? Is your friend's happiness of no interest to you?" Elizabeth's voice bristled with frustration. "I know not why this comes as a surprise. You have always viewed my family with disdain. You barely tolerate my presence."

"That is not true." He ran his long fingers through his dark hair. "I admire you, regardless of what I may think of your relatives. Why would you think otherwise?"

Elizabeth sat back in her chair and looked at him point-blank. "Does, 'she is tolerable though not handsome enough to tempt me,' sound familiar?"

He rose from his seat. Unhurried, he walked towards the fireplace. He turned to face her. "I supposed you had overheard me, though I never knew for certain. This is my sole excuse for not apologising. I am sorry I ever uttered those words. I did not mean them at the time. Without question, those words do not describe my sentiments now. The truth is—"

Darcy halted his speech. Elizabeth caught a glimpse of something in his face, what seemed an air of longing. She had witnessed it many times when gentlemen looked at Jane. What might it mean if she had more than tempted him? Perchance his look was one of adoration. But how could it be? Mr. Darcy never looked at her, even once, except to find fault.

"The truth is what, Mr. Darcy?"

"Never mind what I was about to say."

"In the letter that Miss Bingley wrote to my sister telling of Mr. Bingley's plans never to return to Hertfordshire, she hinted of an attachment between Miss Darcy and Mr. Bingley.

Can this be true?"

Darcy raised his eyebrow. Elizabeth's muscles tightened. He was questioning her audacity!

"If it is not true, why would you allow such falsehoods to be spread about your young sister? Miss Bingley told Jane. Surely, she would tell others when it suited her purposes."

Darcy walked to the window. He said nothing.

"You need not confirm nor deny Caroline's assertions, Mr. Darcy. From what Mr. Wickham told me of your sister, I find it difficult to believe she would even consider an alliance with Mr. Bingley."

Catching his breath, he turned to face her. "Wickham? I trust you are not taking your cues on human behaviour from the likes of him!" Darcy rolled his eyes in displeasure. "What is this power he holds over gullible, unsuspecting young women?"

"Gullible? Unsuspecting? You dare to accuse me of such measly traits, merely because I chose to befriend a perfectly amiable gentleman who makes himself agreeable wherever he goes, whilst you, sir, are content to give offence to anyone whom you deem beneath you!"

He raised both hands in mocked surrender. "If the shoe fits—"

Insufferable man! Elizabeth rubbed her temple. The throbbing headache she had suffered whilst in Miss Bingley's company was returning. Her gaze drifted past him to the world outside. All had quieted. Elizabeth's eyes darted towards the mantle clock. Time had passed quickly. She had not planned to be away from her relatives' home so long. She surmised she had better take her leave rather than argue with the stubborn man who stood before her. She had grown tired by now, owing to more than her present company. Unlike the night before, she supposed she would have little trouble finding sleep when she laid her head to rest that evening.

Elizabeth arose to her feet. She cleared her scratchy throat. "I realise what you are about, Mr. Darcy. You do not intend to help me. You merely intend to taunt and bait me, knowing where any discussion between the two of us on the subject of Mr. Wickham leads. An ensuing argument will pacify your guilty conscience for refusing to help reunite Mr. Bingley and my sister!"

Darcy looked more surprised, or amused, rather than offended. This upset Elizabeth even more. Any disappointment she suffered, she directed towards herself. She had taken her chance with him and failed miserably.

"Good-bye, Mr. Darcy." Elizabeth walked to the door and grasped its handle. "I feel it is more than I owe, but it would be rude of me not to thank you for your time."

What had started as light inconvenient drops of rain as Elizabeth made her way down the stairs of Darcy House soon gave way to buckets of water pouring from the sky when she stepped on the footway. Already damp from the earlier downpour, her hooded cloak was her sole protection.

Where is the hackney coach? She had asked the driver to return for her in under an hour. *Has he come and gone?* She prayed another would happen along soon. Her cloak was no match for the harsh rain. Already she felt the rain seeping through.

Before she knew it, the tall dark figure she espied from the corner of her eye loomed over her, holding a large black umbrella. Despite the reprieve from the pounding rain against her face afforded by the protective cover, she did not bless its bearer with any measure of charity.

"I do not need to tell you that you should not be standing out in this weather." He, too, shivered from the brutal elements' chill. "This is ridiculous. Please, come back inside." By now, he was shouting.

"No!" Elizabeth cried back above the deafening rain. What would have been the point in returning inside with him when he only meant to mock her? He certainly did not mean to help her. The sooner her hired coach returned, the sooner she might fend for herself.

"Why are you even standing here?" His elevated voice barely resonated over the rain's fierce drumming. "I assure you the chances of a passing coach are minuscule."

"I have made arrangements, Mr. Darcy. My coach will return for me."

"Then where is it? Come inside. I shall arrange for your safe return to Cheapside once my valet returns with my carriage."

She pretended not to hear his magnanimous offer. *I would never allow such a thing. What might my uncle and aunt think in beholding such an indecorous spectacle?*

At last, her carriage, no—not *her* carriage, but a carriage, nonetheless, rounded the corner. Elizabeth stepped forward, nearer to the curb. Darcy stepped forward, as well, attempting to keep her sheltered by his umbrella. Elizabeth held out her hand in vain. The coachman had no intention of stopping, making avoidance of what was to come impossible. Swished puddles of street water splattered the two of them from head to toe.

Chapter 4

Darcy and Elizabeth were drenched. He tossed his umbrella aside, and along with it, any semblance of propriety, and took Elizabeth by the hand. Together, they raced up the stairs. Dripping water along the fine flooring and the exquisite carpets of Darcy House, they did not stop until they were once again standing before the warm fire in Darcy's study.

Darcy stood before Elizabeth and stared into her eyes an endless moment.

"Let me take your wet cloak and settle you by the fire."

She offered no objection. Her teeth chattered as a result of the cold seeping through her body. Brushing her hand aside, he started unfastening her cloak, as if mindless of the impropriety, as if thinking only of her needs.

Before she could voice her protest aloud, he lowered her sopping-wet cloak from her shoulders and tossed it aside. The street water on top of the pouring rain had soaked through her outer garment, leaving Elizabeth's day dress wet. Her petticoats were sodden, as well. Darcy quickly removed his greatcoat.

Next, he removed his jacket and placed it about her shoulders in a manner intimating his pressing desire to shelter her. Grateful for its warmth, Elizabeth clutched the lapels together and sat on the settee. The pleasant hint of masculinity lingered in the garment. She found his jacket arousing, yet comforting, and did not resist the temptation to breathe in its cosiness.

Darcy filled a fresh snifter with brandy. Returning to her side, he handed her the glass. "Drink this. It will warm you from the inside."

Elizabeth eyed the glass and frowned. She feared the aroma might just as likely bring on a bout of nausea. The last thing in the world she needed was to fall ill in his home. Darcy removed it from her hand. His fingers lingered about hers for a moment. Elizabeth found it all rather confusing, the discordance of her body and her mind. The wet clothes clinging to her body did not help, but somehow his attentions were calming. "What may I offer you? You must drink something warm. Your voice sounds raspy. Would you enjoy a cup of tea?"

"You said no servants are in the house." Elizabeth swallowed, soothing her aching throat. "I do not mean to put you to any trouble, Mr. Darcy."

"Do you think me incapable of preparing a pot of tea, madam?"

Elizabeth did not respond. Her expression said everything.

"Very well then; I must prove my domestic prowess."

Darcy reached across Elizabeth's shoulder, in a most intimate manner, and retrieved the blanket she had seen earlier. "May I?" he said as he replaced his jacket with it. His jacket, she noticed, was nearly soaked through. "I believe you will find this more comfortable." He gently wrapped the blanket about her shoulders. "Stay here and warm yourself by the fire.

I shall be back in no time at all."

Darcy stood to quit the room. Hesitating at the door, he turned and looked back. "Promise me that you will await my return."

After nodding her assent, Elizabeth found herself alone in his study, reflecting on the unexpected turn of events.

My day was not supposed to turn out this way. Elizabeth shivered before the fire. How she longed to remove her muslin gown and a few other unmentionables to wring them by hand. That is exactly what she would have done, if she had thought she could manage it before Mr. Darcy returned from the kitchen.

His opinion of me must certainly sink should he return and find me standing in his study nearly undressed. Elizabeth took her shoes off and placed them on the hearth to dry. Surely, he would have no objections. Feeling a bit too weak to continue standing, Elizabeth wrapped herself in the blanket again and returned to the settee.

It simply cannot be helped. I must remove my wet clothing. When Mr. Darcy returns, I shall request the privacy of another room that I might disrobe whilst my dress dries by the fire. Otherwise ... otherwise, I might catch my death of cold.

Shivering, Elizabeth rested her head on one of the pillows. Her weary body moaned. For her aching muscles, she blamed the lost battle she had waged in her quest for sleep the night before. Now it had caught up with her.

Today has been the worst day of my life.

ಬಿಬಿಬಿ

Darcy entered the room bearing a silver tray laden with cups, sugar, cream, and tea, as well as a tea urn filled with hot water. Setting up for tea was more trouble than he had imagined. It had taken a bit longer than he had thought, but he was pleased with the outcome. It would have taken even longer had his valet not anticipated his needs and laid everything out. He had even prepared the fire. All Darcy had needed to do was boil the water. Mindful his guest might be hungry, he regretted his inability to offer her anything of sustenance, not even a piece of bread. Darcy set the tea service on the side table the same way as he had witnessed his staff performing their duties. He poured a cup.

"How do you take your tea, Miss Elizabeth?"

Silence.

Darcy turned to face Elizabeth and noticed her shoes arranged by the fireplace hearth to dry. She lay curled up on the couch; her hair, now loosened, cascaded over the cover, her stocking feet peeked from underneath.

He returned the cup to the tray and walked to the settee. "Miss Elizabeth."

No answer. He knelt beside her.

"Miss Elizabeth," he said softly. Though her hair was nearly dry, beads of sweat had replaced what had been remnants of raindrops along the edges of her hairline. He placed the back of his hand to her forehead. Its shocking warmth startled him.

"Please, open your eyes ... Miss Elizabeth."

His hushed bidding slowly awakened her. "Mr. Darcy?"

"Yes, I am here. You fell asleep."

She slowly managed to sit up. The blanket was nearly as wet as her dress by now. "I hate to impose ... any more than I have, sir, but ... I must—"

"Yes, you must remove your wet things. I will show you to another room."

With some trouble, Elizabeth stood, unsteadily. Darcy took her by her elbow.

"Are you certain you are all right? You look—"

Elizabeth endeavoured to take a step on her own. "Yes, I shall be—" She collapsed into Darcy's strong, waiting arms. His cool demeanour tempered what might have been cause for panic. He needed to get her into bed, and then summon his physician. If only his valet would return with the carriage!

Darcy glanced at the mantle clock. *Where is Waters? He should have returned by now. What is keeping him?*

With Elizabeth now securely in his arms, Darcy beheld the rise and fall of her chest. *The next several hours will tell the tale. I shall keep watch over her.*

ঙওঙও

"Is Lizzy planning to join us for dinner this evening?" Mr. Gardiner said. A man of sense and fortitude, he was the younger brother of Elizabeth's mother. Through his industrious efforts, he managed a profitable business in Cheapside. He worked hard, and as always, a long day in one of his warehouses found him ravenous for a hearty evening meal.

"I do not suppose she will. I have sent a tray up to her room. Poor thing, I went up to check on her earlier. My light knocks went unanswered." Mrs. Gardiner set her sewing aside. "I supposed she was fast asleep. Mrs. North prepared a special tea for her that she might rest better. I did not have the heart to enter the room and risk disturbing her after her restless night."

"Yes, I understand she has been a godsend in helping to care for the children since her arrival from Longbourn, but I reckon their sufferings have been passed on to her."

"I tend to agree. I pray a full day's rest has made a difference in restoring her health. She has been cooped up in this house for too long, and you know how she enjoys long walks."

"I do indeed, though I dare say a long walk in Cheapside hardly compares to one of her countryside rambles in Hertfordshire."

"I agree. This might explain why she has not often ventured out-of-doors. Shall we proceed to the dining room for dinner?"

"Yes." Mr. Gardiner's stomach voiced its concurrence with loud rumblings. Chuckling, he patted his belly. "By the way, my dear, how was your visit with Lady Susan?"

"The visit was delightful; though, she was rather distressed our niece was unable to accompany me. She looks forward to making Lizzy's acquaintance."

"Yes, of course. She continues to be of a mind to take Lizzy under her wing for the Season, does she not?"

"Indeed, she does. What a good thing for our Lizzy, do you not agree? Who knows? Lady Susan may be of assistance to our sister in helping find a husband for one of her daughters."

"Let us take one step at a time, my dear. One step at a time—" The housemaid appeared from around the corner, interrupting his speech. "Betsy, how did you find my dear niece?"

"Yes, Betsy, did Lizzy have anything to eat?"

"No ma'am—" Betsy's countenance revealed her exhaustion and dismay.

"Why in heaven not? She must eat something." Mrs. Gardiner turned to her husband. "You go ahead. I shall join you after looking in on Lizzy."

"I beg your pardon, ma'am. Miss Elizabeth is not in her room. I looked everywhere." Betsy wrung her hands together nervously. "She is nowhere to be found."

෩෩෩

Darcy carried Elizabeth upstairs. With the size of the house and the lack of staff, save his valet, he determined it best to put Elizabeth in the room next to his … the mistress's suite. That way, he would be near her throughout the night. He found the room colder than he thought advisable and opted instead to carry her into his room and lay her upon his bed, whilst he laid a fire in the adjoining apartment. He had no wish to leave her alone in such a feverish state, not even long enough to prepare the room. He had no other choice.

He resisted the temptation to run his fingers through her

loosened hair. Dark, cascading the expanse of her shoulders and down her back, he had seen it thus several times in Hertfordshire, the first time being the day she walked three miles from Longbourn to Netherfield Park. Her eyes, brightened by the exercise, had cast a spell upon him. Not a day had passed since that day that he had not thought of her.

He once again recalled Elizabeth's penchant for walking, a sign of her strong constitution in his estimation. Seeing her as such, he prayed she had not succumbed to some dreadful illness. *Perhaps the foul air of Cheapside has led to her malaise or maybe it was the exposure to the cold rain.*

He covered her with a bed cloth. "Rest here whilst I prepare the other room. I shall not take long."

Having prepared the fire as well as venturing to his sister's room to secure night clothing, he returned to his room. Elizabeth had not stirred. Her breathing remained uneasy, heightening his anxiety over the extent of her discomfort. He carried her through the adjoining door between his room and the mistress's suite and laid her upon the bed.

"Please forgive me for this horrible breach in decorum, Miss Elizabeth.

"I have placed you in the room adjacent to my own. In case you should stir during the night, awaken, and find yourself in a strange and unfamiliar environment, you will find me on the other side of the door.

"We are hardly strangers, you and I. Did we not spend several nights under the same roof in Hertfordshire?

"Now, I must get you out of your wet clothing." Darcy sat on the bed next to her.

"Forgive me," he whispered as he began the meticulous tasks of a lady's maid.

An hour later, Darcy stood outside the apartment door talking with his valet in hushed whispers. Having seen to the task of notifying essential household staff of the master's early return to town as well as seeing to it that they assumed their posts immediately, the valet awaited his next assignment.

"Once you have notified my physician of the situation, speak with my solicitor. Surely, he will know how to contact Mr. Gardiner. The Gardiners must be informed of their niece's condition as soon as possible."

"Yes, Mr. Darcy. Is there anything more I might do?"

"Bingley will be at the club by now. Meet him there and make my excuses."

"What shall I tell him, sir?"

"Tell him that I am otherwise engaged." Darcy frowned. "Tell him that I will make it up to him tomorrow."

"If you will pardon my asking, sir, what should Miss Darcy be told of your desire for her to return to your home ahead of schedule?"

"Tell her that I need her, as soon as can be."

The valet's conflicted countenance recalled Darcy to the delicate nature of his predicament. No doubt, his relatives, Lord and Lady Matlock, would have many questions when Waters arrived at their doorstep. "My aunt and uncle must know nothing of this situation. I shall rely upon your good judgment."

೮೦೮೦೮೦

Elizabeth stirred. Her mind clouded. *I must leave here. My aunt and uncle will be worried.* She noted the rich fabric of her gown, the soft bed, the smoothing fragrance of chamomile, the warmth of the fire.

I shall lie here for another five minutes. Certainly, no more than ten.

Hours later, Elizabeth awakened with the sense of having been trapped in the midst of sleep and near consciousness, yet with a strange notion of having been cared for ... a strong yet tender voice hushing her coughs, a gentle hand resting upon her own. She opened her eyes and slowly took in her surroundings. The majestic room had not been a figment of her dreams. An opened book on the bedside table confirmed her suspicions of having been watched over. A maid scurrying about caught Elizabeth's notice. Had she been the one who cared for her? Once again, she wrapped herself in sleep's warm embrace.

Later still, the moistened cloth dabbing her forehead, her cheeks, and along her neckline soothed her hot skin. Elizabeth opened her eyes.

"Good morning, milady."

Elizabeth lifted her head from the pillow. The magnificent drapes, the rich mahogany poster bed, and the fine silken sheets—every corner of the room whispered opulence. No, she had not been dreaming. Her chest hurt. Her fog-filled head and sore throat notwithstanding, she whispered, "Where am I?"

"You are in the mistress's suite, milady."

"Who are you?"

"My name is Anna. I am Miss Darcy's maid. You gave us quite a scare. The master's physician said your collapse last evening was due to fever. How do you feel this morning?"

"I—" Elizabeth began coughing.

"Please, milady, do not strain yourself. I shall fetch some hot tea. I shall only be a moment."

"No, no. I must go. I must—"

"Pardon my saying so, but I fear you are in no condition to go anywhere."

"I cannot remain here. My aunt will be worried."

"Do not fret. Miss Darcy mentioned that your aunt is bringing some of your things around this morning. Everything is arranged."

"My aunt is coming here? She cannot discover me here." Elizabeth fingered the sleeve of her exquisite nightgown. "Where is my clothing? I must dress. She cannot find me here."

Anna did as told and aided Elizabeth in dressing. Moments later, a young woman of Elizabeth's height and figure and the face of an angel entered the room.

"Miss Elizabeth? Why are you out of bed?"

Elizabeth eyed the young lady with circumspection.

"Forgive me. I am Georgiana Darcy. I looked in on you earlier this morning. I did not expect to find you up and about."

"Miss Darcy," she began slowly. The exertion of dressing, even with Anna's assistance, had drained her energy. Elizabeth sat down. "I appreciate your kindness. Anna said that my aunt is arriving with some of my things. I had much rather she did not find me here. I would rather meet her in the drawing room."

"You are not well. You had much better return to bed and get some rest."

"I cannot rest ... not here ... in—"

"The mistress's suite," Anna completed Elizabeth's sentiments in a tone conveying concurrence.

"Very well, Miss Elizabeth." Georgiana turned her attention to Anna. "I hate to impose upon you, but with the absence of so many staff, will you see that the Blue bedroom is prepared for the remainder of Miss Elizabeth's stay."

"Yes, ma'am." She curtsied and left the room.

"That is not necessary. I doubt I will remain here."

A light tap at the door drew their attention.

"Miss Darcy, Mrs. Gardiner has arrived. She is in the drawing room."

"Thank you, Mr. Hart."

Upon his leave-taking, Georgiana placed her hand upon Elizabeth's. "Are you certain you are up to receiving your aunt downstairs?"

"I am afraid I have no other choice. May we proceed?"

Elizabeth smiled through the nagging muscle aches rendered by the long journey from the mistress's suite to the drawing room. Georgiana released her grip of Elizabeth's arm and walked over to greet her guest.

"Mrs. Gardiner, welcome to my brother's home. I am Georgiana Darcy."

"Miss Darcy, it is a pleasure to meet you. I must tell you how relieved I was to hear from you and your brother regarding my niece." She walked to Elizabeth. "You gave us quite a scare last evening, my dear. Why in heaven are you out of bed?"

"You must not fuss over me. I assure you my appearance belies how I actually feel." Elizabeth did not miss their exchanged doubtful looks.

"Come, sit by the fire. You will find it comfortable there," said Mrs. Gardiner.

"Yes, please have a seat. Tea should arrive momentarily."

The warm blazing fire, tea, Mr. Darcy's jacket ... the events of the evening before were coming back to her. She had drifted asleep on the settee. How might everything since that moment be explained?

Where is Mr. Darcy? He and I were alone by his account. How did I find myself in bed ... dressed in such fine bed clothing? Embarrassed, confused, Elizabeth felt the colour drain from her face.

"My dear Lizzy, I fear you should not be up and about. I insist you return to bed."

"Although I will admit feeling somewhat poorly, I will manage." She looked at Miss Darcy. "Again, I appreciate your kindness." Elizabeth turned to her aunt. "I would like to return to Cheapside, as soon as can be."

"I dare not argue with you, though I would much rather not risk your health by exposing you to the outside elements for any considerable length of time."

"You fail to understand! I must leave. I promise I shall rest once we are home."

Once again, Elizabeth discerned their mutual scepticism, only this time laced with resignation.

"I shall call for the carriage," Georgiana said.

∞∞∞

Darcy found his sister in the drawing room upon his return. "Have you visited Miss Elizabeth this morning? Is she resting?"

"Miss Elizabeth is not here."

Her words struck him like a punch in the stomach. "Not here?"

"When her aunt, Mrs. Gardiner, arrived this morning with her things, Miss Elizabeth insisted she was well enough to return to the Gardiners' home."

"I find that difficult to conceive." Darcy endeavoured to mask his disappointment. *She suffered a fitful sleep most of the night.* "How did you find her? Is she truly recovered … enough to travel across town?"

"That, I cannot say." She placed her hand on his. "Miss Elizabeth was adamant she should return to her relatives' home rather than remain here at Darcy House. She is safe from harm, Brother. You need not fret. I believe it is for the best that she should be allowed to recuperate amongst her loved ones."

Darcy smiled warily.

"With your permission, I shall call on Miss Elizabeth in a day or two. Try not to worry." She lifted herself upon her toes and kissed his chiselled chin before quitting the room.

His sister was right. Elizabeth's leaving his home before he had a chance to say or do something he might regret was for the best. Would to heaven that those words held sway over his wounded heart.

Chapter 5

Lady Gwendolen Helmsley sat across the table from her brother. She had outdone herself as the lady of the house again. By all accounts, the party was heralded a success. The usual friends and aristocratic family members had been in attendance: Lord and Lady Langley; Lord and Lady Hathaway; Sir Lewis Downing and his wife, Mildred; Mr. Darcy; and lastly, the enchanting young widow, Juliette, Duchess of Sexton. Lord Latham would have it no other way; insisting that if the Duchess were not in attendance, there would be no party. Lady Gwendolen had protested as usual. She did not like Her Grace for some odd reason she could never quite make out. Indeed, she had done her part, even going out of her way to make the Duchess feel welcomed.

Now, if only her brother would do his part. He and Fitzwilliam Darcy were best friends after all … had been for years. As much as she esteemed her role as the hostess in her brother's home, she wanted more. She longed to be mistress of her own home, mistress of Pemberley.

Her ladyship tapped her fingers and blew out her breath,

gently disturbing the loose strands of hair crowning her forehead, as well as one rather bothered earl.

Lord Latham laid his paper aside. "I grant you my undivided attention, my lady."

"At last, his lordship deigns to acknowledge the presence of his *favourite* sister."

"My *only* sister."

She ignored his jest for she knew she was more than his favourite sister. He had said many times that she was his favourite person in the world. They were inseparable. Her senior by seven years, he had been more a parent to her than a brother, even though fewer than four years had passed since they lost their mother and father.

"Have you heard from Mr. Darcy? What are his plans for the Season?"

"He was our guest for three weeks. Surely, you were able to use your feminine wiles to your advantage and glean such information for yourself."

"Please, Trevor, do not patronise me. He treated me as your little sister, much the same as when you first brought him home during the holiday all those years ago."

"I dare say you are mistaken."

"What? Oh, Trevor, you must not tease me today. Tell me what he said, please. Heaven knows he barely utters a word to me."

"Let us say he is mindful of my feelings as regards an alliance between our families. I did champion you."

"How? What did you say, brother? I must know."

"I told him you are the opposite of the women he abhors as evident by your shy demeanour around him. Although I have explained how lively and gay you are when he is absent. I reminded him that you are now fully grown and an accomplished woman with beauty and a fortune of your own. You would enhance his status, and I would welcome him as a brother. However, his response is such that I dare not discuss. Darcy is my friend and confidant." He patted her hand.

"Please, Trevor. I must know if I have a chance. Do not tease me."

He placed his hand upon her arm. "Please, dearest, have patience. Darcy will come around."

"So he does not want me." She sighed. Her shoulders fell.

"You will have your Mr. Darcy."

"How?"

"I shall continue to take every opportunity to remind him that you are the only choice he could ever possibly make for a wife. Does that satisfy your ladyship?"

Lady Gwendolen stood from her chair and waltzed to her brother's side. Delighted by his news, she kissed his strong, sculpted chin. She could always count on him.

ଚ୍ଚଚ୍ଚ

"Miss Darcy bestowed a great kindness in calling on you," Mrs. Gardiner said as she began fussing over her niece, straightening the bed covers around Elizabeth's waist, fluffing and rearranging the pillows, and the like.

"Indeed." Elizabeth's tone suggested she still did not know what to make of the visit. Miss Darcy had shown none of the haughtiness of her brother, which Mr. Wickham had ascribed to her. *Perhaps he had described her as she had been during a more trying time of youth.*

"It speaks highly of Mr. Darcy, as well, to have sent his personal physician to attend you."

"Yes, Mr. Darcy is the epitome of kindness."

Mrs. Gardiner raised her eyebrow. "Far different from the man whom Mr. Wickham described when we were introduced in Hertfordshire, I might add."

"I am not totally resolved against Mr. Wickham's account, I am afraid. Yes, Mr. Darcy sent his physician to check on my health. That speaks as much to his wealth as to his goodness as a human being." In Elizabeth's opinion, were Mr. Darcy truly concerned for her welfare, he might have come himself, rather than send his sister as his surrogate. Not that she wanted to see him.

"I caution you, Lizzy, not to think too fondly of Mr. Wickham's opinion and too poorly of Mr. Darcy's, a man one hundred times the lieutenant's worth. Mind you, I speak of more than his fortune."

"You sound like Charlotte, for she uttered words along a similar vein. However, for reasons I care not to discuss, I am inclined to disagree. Mr. Wickham is worth more than all the Mr. Darcys in the world." Elizabeth smiled at her outrageous sentiments, knowing full well that such a thing was improbable—a sure sign as any of the return of her good spirits.

"Lizzy, I am glad your health is recovered. I want to discuss a particular matter with you."

"What matter is that?"

"Well, Lizzy, obviously Miss Darcy and you have no prior acquaintance. You do not even like Mr. Darcy. How did you come to be in his home ... all the way across town?"

"My dear aunt, please do not think me foolish. I know my behaviour in going to Mr. Darcy's home was unconscionable. I offer no excuse except my love for my sister demanded I go. Jane is as miserable now as she was over Christmas.

"You must remember how she comported herself, refusing to join in the celebration of the season with the rest of the family." Elizabeth cradled her knees to her chest. "Mr. Bingley's abandonment rendered her heart-broken. Things grew worse when she received a letter from Miss Caroline Bingley saying they were not to return to Hertfordshire, not for the winter, perhaps not ever. She even hinted of an alliance between Miss Darcy and Mr. Bingley as the reason. Jane is devastated."

"What a shame. I am sorry to hear how awful things are. Perhaps, Lizzy, that explains your sullen reception of Miss Darcy. It does not explain why, or even how, you found yourself in her brother's home."

"I had not intended to call on Mr. Darcy. I initially called on Miss Bingley, with the hope of seeing Mr. Bingley, as well. All she did was expound on her earlier lies and even compounded them by saying her brother was not in town." Elizabeth gave her aunt a full account of the visit. Commencing upon an explanation of the subsequent events, she said, "I knew from our past acquaintance in Hertfordshire that Mr. Darcy lived nearby, I knew not where, but I was able to find out with the assistance of the coachman. As with Miss Bingley, I saw no harm in calling on Miss Darcy with the hope of gaining an audience with her brother." Her account might have suffered a bit of embellishment. However, Miss Darcy had not let on that she was not in residence at her brother's home at the time of Elizabeth's arrival; Elizabeth saw no need to alter that perception. "I wanted to find out for myself the truth of Miss Bingley's assertions that her brother was out of town. I also went there to ask for his assistance in persuading Mr. Bingley of Jane's love for him."

"Nothing would come of my scolding you now on the indecorous manner in which you chose to help Jane. I ask only that you think better of what you are about before taking on such an endeavour again." After a moment, Mrs. Gardiner touched Elizabeth's chin. "I take it by your low opinion of Mr. Darcy that he did not heed your request for his assistance."

"Indeed, he did not, so I wasted my time. He will not help. He said as much." Elizabeth frowned. She crossed her arms. "I am exceedingly vexed. What is more, I failed to discern whether Miss Darcy and Mr. Bingley are attached. I asked Mr. Darcy directly, and he refused to answer.

"From what I have seen of Miss Darcy, I cannot conceive how it might be true. She is far too young to entertain notions of marriage. If anything, I suspect Mr. Darcy is more interested in having Mr. Bingley as a brother than Miss Darcy is interested in having Mr. Bingley as a husband."

Mrs. Gardiner smiled. "It seems you have everything figured out." She stood and prepared to leave. "Please, rest now. Remember, Lady Susan is joining us for dinner tomorrow. She is most anxious to meet you. By the way, have you thought about her proposal?"

Elizabeth's countenance spoke to her lack of resolve towards Lady Susan's scheme. She had yet to meet her, and thus no basis for feeling one way or another. Besides, Elizabeth had but a single purpose in being in town. Her aunt had no way of knowing that when she first agreed to propose the scheme to Elizabeth.

"Truth be told, Lizzy," Mrs. Gardiner said, "I suppose Lady Susan is lonely. She is seeking to reintroduce herself into society since the death of her husband; therefore, she has extended this invitation. It will give her some sense of purpose, if you will."

"Why me? I have no interest in being a paid companion."

"Who said anything of the kind? I assure you her intention is not to hire you. You are a gentleman's daughter. You would be as much a companion to Lady Susan as she would be a companion to you."

Mrs. Gardiner turned to leave the room. "You need not make your decision now, Lizzy. Meet Lady Susan and decide for yourself if you are interested in spending time with her over the coming weeks."

Elizabeth considered her aunt's words carefully. Lady Susan would surely travel amongst the highest circles of Society. She would no doubt have an opportunity to see Mr. Bingley. *Why did I not think of this before? Indeed, Lady Susan's invi-*

tation is the answer to my dilemma.

ಙಢಙಢಙಢ

The next evening, Elizabeth sat at the dressing table, preparing her hair and looking into the mirror, searching her memory for answers she was not even sure she wanted. The reflexion of the untouched cup of tea on her bedside table unsettled her. She had acquired a decided dislike of tea of late. Unable to explain it, she surmised she had better get over it, for she would sooner give up breathing than stop having tea.

Elizabeth furrowed her brow. Not knowing what may or may not have happened at Mr. Darcy's home was a matter she found hard to reconcile. It bothered her.

Why am I unable to recall anything? Flummoxed, she pushed such worries aside and deliberated instead upon her latest scheme. She liked this new plan, for it would surely put her in Mr. Bingley's path.

Of course, travelling in the same circles as Mr. Bingley meant she might also come across Mr. Darcy. *What must it be like seeing him again?* Elizabeth frowned. *Why am I always thinking of him?* She sought a distraction. She removed a recent letter from her dressing table drawer and read it for a second time.

My dear Lizzy,

To answer the question that must surely be uppermost in your mind, Jane fares no better, but no worse, preferring still to pass the bulk of her time in solitary.

As promised, I have said nothing to her of your plans. With that being said, in no way do I pardon your decision to seek out the gentleman from Netherfield Park to ascertain the workings of his heart as regards our eldest sister. I, like Jane, believe his actions speak to his purposes.

My feelings on the matter, however, in no way preclude my curiosity in hearing of your success in your undertaking to unmask the well-concealed sentiments of said gentleman's mind. Have you had occasion to meet with him, to speak with him?

Pray do not keep me in suspense, as I will endeavour to sate your curiosity over the comings and goings here. Your place at our dinner table, as well as Jane's, I regretfully add, are often enjoyed by the dashing (Lydia's words, not mine) Mr. Wickham and his friend Mr. Denny, instead. The gentlemen are determined to make Longbourn their home away from home, giving Mama, Lydia, and Kitty as much satisfaction as anyone who knows of their adulation of a red coat might expect. Papa's sentiments are not as easily discerned. He spends more time in his library now than ever before.

The first hints of spring have heightened our youngest sisters' enthusiasm for walking to Meryton every day with the anticipated delight of returning with the aforementioned gentlemen. I am reminded of Fordyce's words in this regard, for men can be forgiven many faults for which no such mercy awaits the female.

Though I shall not be accused of gossiping, it is said that the sudden acquisition of ten thousand pounds has embellished the most remarkable charms of Miss King, the young lady to whom Mr. Wickham renders himself exceedingly agreeable. Whilst I know you are apt to think rather fondly of the gentleman, I can only wonder where he finds the time to spread his prettiness as thin as he does.

You now have the whole of it. Before closing, I shall take this opportunity to remind you to be careful in your pursuit of true love and happiness on our eldest sister's behalf.

Your loving sister,
Mary

As satisfied as she could be with Mary's account of Jane, Elizabeth folded the letter and placed it in the top drawer of her dressing table. She soon found herself mulling over other snippets.

One can hardly blame Mr. Wickham for his attentiveness to Miss King. I shall not fault him one bit. So what if he does marry her with the prospect of controlling her fortune of ten thousand pounds? Would that render him any less a good husband? I think not!

Thoughts of Mr. Wickham's fate gave way to thoughts of his nemesis, the man who had wronged him and had thought little of doing so. *Had Mr. Darcy honoured the dictates of the elder Mr. Darcy's will, and given Mr. Wickham the living in Kympton that he ought to have had, none of this would be happening. Rather than a poor lieutenant with little to offer, he would be a suitable husband for any woman.* Elizabeth smiled in fond remembrance of the gentleman. *Indeed, I hope he finds happiness with Miss King.*

He has been a true friend, and he was right about the haughty gentleman from Derbyshire.

"Mr. Darcy," Elizabeth said aloud. "What a waste of my time and efforts."

She resolved she would have no ally in Mr. Darcy. *After what occurred in his home, is it any wonder he has no wish to see me?* Elizabeth cocked her head to the side and studied her reflexion.

What exactly did happen? One minute I was sitting by the fire; next thing I found myself awakening in the mistress's suite.

Elizabeth looked around her bedchamber. *The apartment was amazing. Ivory coloured curtains with precious interwoven strands of gold, awe-inspiring paintings, richly sculptured mahogany furniture. To be mistress of such a place would be something.*

Elizabeth returned her gaze to her mirror. She ran her fingers along the sleeve of her muslin gown. How many times had she worn it? *Miss Darcy's gown looked as if it had never been worn before that day.* Elizabeth sighed. *I would not wish for a thousand such gowns, not if it meant being associated with Mr. Darcy. He is far more arrogant than I ever suspected during our initial acquaintance.*

She creased her brow and rested her hand on her cheek. *Of course, he did apologise for his rudeness at the Meryton assembly; I remember that much. He said he admired me. He took my hand in his, and we ran up the stairs to escape the rain ... and then, when—*

Elizabeth chastised herself for her romantic musings. *What am I thinking? Mr. Darcy flatly refused to help me. I declare, I cannot abide the haughty man.*

"I do not believe he did not come here to check on my welfare for himself!" Elizabeth said aloud.

ॐॐॐ

Darcy looked in on his sister in the music room practising on the pianoforte. As soon as she paused for a brief rest, he raised the question that had plagued his mind all morning.

"How was your visit with Miss Elizabeth, Georgiana? Pray tell she fares much better."

"Yes, Brother, Miss Elizabeth's health is recovering nicely."

"Did she enjoy the fresh flowers and fruit?"

"I suppose so. She seemed delighted by the gesture. However, I must admit she was rather quiet. Odd, I did not take her for being shy."

Elizabeth is hardly shy. I hope she does not view my sister as an impediment to her sister's prospects.

Georgiana stood from the pianoforte and cajoled him to sit with her. "Brother, you must admit I have been exceedingly patient through all this. I believe I deserve answers. Do you not agree?"

"Answers? To what are you referring, Georgiana?"

"Oh, I speak of this entire affair with Miss Elizabeth Bennet. You have yet to give me a full account of how she came to be in our mother's room."

"Georgiana, I have told you nearly everything there is to tell. Miss Elizabeth fell ill whilst visiting me. I had no choice but to tend to her needs as best I could, what with the entire staff out of the house."

"But why was she even here? You have to admit it is not entirely proper."

"True, it is not proper, but to be honest, Miss Elizabeth is known for doing what she wants to do when she wants to, especially when it comes to matters of importance to her."

"Why do I suspect you like that about her?" Georgiana said. He recalled how often he spoke of Elizabeth in his letters from Hertfordshire, thus suffered no surprise by his sister's supposition.

"I confess. I admire Miss Elizabeth a great deal. However, she came here because she wanted a favour of me, a favour I am not inclined to bestow."

"Brother, what type of request would bring a young woman from across town, and why would you deny her, especially if you admire her, as you say you do?"

Darcy took his sister's hand and squeezed it. The truth was he did not fault Caroline Bingley for having spread the false rumour of a possible alliance between his sister and Charles Bingley. How many times had he secretly wished for the same, especially after her experience in Ramsgate with George Wickham?

"The situation is complicated. I will only say that Miss Elizabeth has her view of certain matters, and I have mine. The two are miles apart. You need not worry on either score.

Chapter 6

Any time he dined at the Hursts' home in Grosvenor Square, it was marked as a momentous occasion, or so it seemed. Miss Caroline Bingley, in all her bright regalia and none too subtle perfumes, sat across the table from him whilst her sister, Louisa, and her sister's husband, Mr. Hurst, sat on either side of him. The only other addition to the party was his friend, Charles Bingley. Indeed, they enjoyed an evening reminiscent of their stay at Netherfield Park months earlier.

"Pray tell, Mr. Darcy, how did you find your stay at Latham Hall?"

"I always enjoy visiting my friend, Lord Latham, Miss Bingley."

"His sister, is she as lovely as ever?" Caroline said. Not that she cared one fig about Lady Gwendolen. Caroline had a keen sense of detecting any woman who had Mr. Darcy in her sights. Darcy would be hard-pressed to pretend he did not notice. Any woman who dared to compete with her in that regard, she detested. How she must have bristled upon learning from Charles that Darcy had joined Lord Latham at his coun-

47

try estate for an extended visit.

"Lady Gwendolen is as she ever was."

"How wonderful! Did she ask after me?"

Darcy raised a befuddled brow. "I beg your pardon?"

"I inquired if Lady Gwendolen asked after me."

"I heard the question. I am confused about your purpose. Even if you and Lady Gwendolen were the best of friends, which I know you are not—I suspect you two are not even acquainted—why would she ask me about you?"

"One commonly receives enquiries on the well-being of one's dearest acquaintances." Darcy cringed inside as a result of the look she bestowed. "Are we not the dearest of acquaintances, Mr. Darcy?" She glanced about the gathering. "I venture our time spent in Hertfordshire made us the closest of friends."

Lips pursed from embarrassment at her sister's forward behaviour, Louisa looked to her husband to rescue the dinner discussion and found an oblivious attendee. He had not peered up from his dish the entire time.

She raised her glass. "I offer a toast to friendship." All save her husband, even the reluctant guest of honour, lifted their glasses. Louisa cleared her throat. "Mr. Hurst!"

For the first time since they sat down to dinner, he gave notice to the others gathered around the table. More aggrieved from being diverted from his meal than embarrassed, he raised his near empty glass. "Yes, my dear. What are we toasting?"

"Caroline remarked on what great friends we became during our stay at Netherfield. We are toasting our friendship."

"Yes, capital! To friendship." He swallowed the deep burgundy wine in a single gulp and signalled the footman for a third refill.

"Speaking of friendships, Caroline, did you not mention

Miss Eliza Bennet's being in town?" Both Darcy and Bingley paused in anticipation of her response. Caroline glared at her sister, for she had obviously spoken out of turn. Darcy wondered how she planned to wiggle her way out of this one.

"May I remind you, dear sister, that I said I have it on good authority from someone in Hertfordshire claiming an acquaintance with me—as though such a thing were possible—that Eliza Bennet is in town? I have not had a chance to see her for myself." Darcy wondered at her mastery of the art of deception.

Louisa's perplexed expression soon relaxed. "Of course, you have not seen her, dear sister."

Caroline smirked. "I dare say our paths will not cross given we do not enjoy the same society."

"You have a point, dear sister."

"Mr. Darcy, what say you? Do you expect we shall enjoy the same society as Eliza Bennet? I recall you thought rather fondly of her fine eyes for a time. You even danced with her during the Netherfield ball. She was the only young woman in Hertfordshire who received such a privilege. Perhaps you might enjoy the prospect of dancing with her again."

"I know of Miss Elizabeth's being in town."

He saw how that bit of news rattled her, and he knew she would rack her poor brain trying to determine how he learned of Elizabeth's being in London. Yet another thing for her to fixate upon.

Bingley sat poised on the edge of his chair. "You know this, Darcy? Have you seen her? Have you spoken with her?"

"Yes, Bingley, in response to each of your questions."

"Why did you not mention this before? Is Miss Bennet in town, as well?"

"Miss Bennet remains in Hertfordshire," Darcy said calmly.

"But Miss Elizabeth is in town. If she is in Cheapside, I

think it might be a good thing to pay her a visit. What say you, Darcy?"

"Heaven forbid, Charles!" Caroline put her napkin aside. "What would be your purpose? Do you go around visiting all the country nothings you have come across in your travels merely because you discover they are in town?"

"I dare say Miss Elizabeth is hardly as you describe, Caroline. She is my neighbour."

"No, Charles, she is the sister of the woman whose family meant to ensnare you. I believe you are the last person Eliza Bennet would wish to see. You know how fiercely protective she is of that family of hers, how shrewish she is. Why subject yourself to her ire?"

"What say you, Darcy?"

"You surely do not need my opinion on those whom you should or should not call upon, Bingley."

"Do you intend to call upon her?"

"Charles, do not be absurd," Louisa said. "Mr. Darcy in Cheapside! I am sure he would sooner set foot in purgatory."

Darcy said nothing, having resolved to stay out of the affair. Bingley might act as he chose as regards visiting Elizabeth, though he prayed he would not. Despite Elizabeth's words to the contrary, he was not persuaded one bit that Jane had fallen in love with his friend on an acquaintance of a few weeks. If his friend found himself the victim of a conniving mama hell-bent on finding a rich husband for her eldest daughter, he would not have him to blame for his ensuing misfortune.

The memory of Elizabeth's enchanting eyes, her lovely lips, her sweet voice, asking, almost begging him for what in her mind was a reasonable request inundated his thoughts. Yet, he would not even consider her entreaties. Not that he doubted his influence over Bingley. More that he suffered no belief in Miss Bennet's sentiments. He had observed her at great length during their last evening at the Netherfield ball. He had detected no special regard on her part towards his friend. What he had observed was a mercenary mama and a malleable daughter. He had seen it before at other places, at other times. Scheming mamas, simpering single daughters, all aimed at his smitten young friend.

Settled in his carriage for a lonely ride to his home, Darcy's thoughts returned to his sister's account of her visit with Elizabeth in Cheapside. It would not do. A single night with her in his home had nearly caused him to toss every argument of reasonableness aside, every notion of familial obligations, and request her hand in marriage.

No. Darcy decided he had got the right of it. Better that he steered clear of Miss Elizabeth Bennet.

ঝঙঝঙ

After dinner, everyone had retired to the Gardiners' drawing room. The tea service was placed, and Mrs. Gardiner poured the first cup and handed it to Lady Susan. Her ladyship, an attractive, middle-aged woman, showed enormous pride in her late sister's only daughter. By her own account, her niece had been such a godsend in the two years since her husband, Lord Townes, had passed away. In the little time she had spent with Elizabeth in her niece's home that evening, she often expressed her appreciation of her niece's deep affection for the younger woman.

"Have you given any thought to my request to spend time with you over the next few weeks?" Lady Susan said.

"I have thought of little else."

"Then what say you?"

"I shall be delighted to be your companion. However, I should like to remain a guest in my aunt and uncle's home."

"I wish you would reconsider, though it shall be no inconvenience to have my carriage at your disposal."

"You are exceedingly generous, your ladyship."

"Indeed." Mrs. Gardiner smiled at her favourite niece and her esteemed aunt. "Well, Lizzy, we have much to do if we are to procure the requisite gowns for your busy social calendar."

"We have little time, my dear. I have accepted an invitation to the Langley Ball. It shall be my chance to introduce you to many of my friends. Fear not, you are sure to meet many pleasant young ladies of your own age. I intend for you to enjoy a glorious time."

Lady Susan graced Mrs. Gardiner with a conspiratorial glance. "I would consider it so much the better if you should meet an agreeable young man in the process."

೮೮೮

Preparing for a ball has never been this time consuming. Elizabeth laid out the dress she had chosen for the evening. Even in a household of five daughters and a single maid between them, it did not take as long. Not that Elizabeth regretted her decision in accepting Lady Susan's invitation. With luck, she might even encounter Mr. Bingley that evening.

Nor did she regret her decision to remain in Cheapside with her aunt and uncle rather than accept the invitation to be a guest in Lady Susan's fashionable Mayfair establishment. Once she had accomplished her mission in ascertaining Mr. Bingley's sentiments towards Jane, she planned to return to Longbourn forthwith.

Elizabeth picked up the emerald-green gown, walked over towards her mirror, and held it up to her slender frame. Her aunt and uncle had been generous in their purchases, but she would not take undue advantage of their kindness. Limiting the number of gowns she had chosen to five, she decided the addition of a shawl, well-placed laces, and various trims would stretch her wardrobe to last a few weeks. The gowns she had

52

brought with her from home would have to suffice for other, informal occasions.

In due time, Lady Susan and Elizabeth stood at the top of the grand staircase at Langley House waiting to be announced. Elizabeth chided herself on her mixture of emotions.

This is ridiculous. I am not a schoolgirl, for heaven's sake. I am nearly one and twenty. If only the flutter in her stomach would cease. *When have I ever been this nervous?*

Indeed, she was uneasy. This was her first occasion to attend such an elaborate soiree. How she wished she had Jane or her dearest friend, Charlotte, by her side.

Upon being announced, they descended the long staircase. Elizabeth wished for a glimpse of anyone she recognised, even Mr. Darcy. Well, no ... not Mr. Darcy. Perhaps Caroline? No, definitely not Caroline. Mr. Bingley? Yes, she prayed he would be in attendance.

Lady Susan interrupted Elizabeth's revelry. "You must not worry, my dear. Everything will be fine. By the end of the evening, you will be the talk of the town."

Elizabeth smiled nervously. The society of Hertfordshire pitted against the pomp of a London *le bon ton* social event, rendered her ill prepared for the evening. The number of single young women seeking husbands surpassed the number of eligible gentlemen in attendance by three. Fortunately, Elizabeth was not to be counted amongst the former; husband hunting, at least for her own sake, was the last thing on her mind. Elizabeth's priority, her greatest hope for the evening, was to encounter Mr. Bingley, with the express purpose of doing what she could to reunite him with her sister.

She suspected Lady Susan might be disappointed with her stance towards marriage. So would her mother, who had given her specific instructions on how to go about winning a husband. Not that Elizabeth begrudged her mother. She had a point. Elizabeth was not getting any younger, and unless she planned to be a spinster, she reckoned she had better start thinking of her own matrimonial prospects. Given the rather limited society in Hertfordshire as well as the fact that she knew every eligible gentleman there, and none, save one, held the slightest bit of interest to her, perhaps staying in London for the remainder of the Season would be in her best interests.

"Elizabeth, my dear, you must stop fretting." Arms linked, Lady Susan and Elizabeth crossed the room to where the dowagers sat.

Soon a distinguished, elderly woman, the mistress of the grand home, joined them. "What a delight it is to see you this evening, my dear Susan. Is this the young lady about whom we have heard?"

"Indeed, Alexandria. I have the pleasure of introducing Miss Elizabeth Bennet of Hertfordshire. Elizabeth, meet Lady Langley."

Elizabeth knew from an earlier discussion with her aunt that Lady Susan's husband, the late Lord Townes, was Lady Alexandria's cousin. Standing proud, a full head above Elizabeth, not counting her elaborate headdress, the Grand Dame observed Elizabeth with thinly disguised curiosity. Elizabeth's courage rose under such scrutiny. She observed Elizabeth from head to toe and smiled, giving Elizabeth the impression that she had been judged and deemed acceptable.

"Welcome to our society, Miss Elizabeth Bennet. I do hope you find everything to your liking."

"I know I shall. Thank you for inviting me, your ladyship."

Lady Susan looked about the exquisitely decorated ballroom. "Now, where is your dear niece? I am anxious to introduce Elizabeth to her, and I am sure Elizabeth is anxious to be amongst the younger ladies, not tucked away in a corner with me."

"My niece is around here somewhere. Better we find her

soon, for it will be quite the crush, and you know how she abhors crowds." She turned to espy an exquisite young woman moving gracefully across the room in their direction.

"Here you are, my dear. Your timing is impeccable," she said upon the young woman's approach.

The younger aristocrat bowed graciously in deference to her elders. "Your ladyships." Dressed in a blue satin gown, complete with brilliant sapphires rivalling her own cerulean blue eyes, she presented a remarkable sight.

"Miss Elizabeth Bennet, I present to you my divine niece, Lady Gwendolen Helmsley."

Both young ladies curtsied. "Miss Bennet, I am pleased to meet you."

"The pleasure is mine, your ladyship."

"Wonderful! Would you care to join me for a glass of punch?"

"Yes, do not let us detain you. You two run along and enjoy yourselves."

The two ladies crossed the room, enjoying light banter along the way.

"I trust you are enjoying yourself this evening, Miss Bennet."

"With pleasure, your ladyship and please, you need only call me Miss Elizabeth."

"Oh, I beg your pardon. Have you many sisters or just the one?"

"I have four sisters, your ladyship. Three are younger."

"I am so terribly jealous, for you see, Miss Elizabeth, I have none. You must tell me about them."

In the next moment, something diverted Lady Gwendolen's attention. Her ladyship laced her arm through Elizabeth's.

"Come, Miss Elizabeth. I wish to introduce you to someone who is rather special to me." The two ladies continued to make their way across the room. There, in the doorway, he stood—tall, dashing, and richly attired in stark black and white.

He greeted them with a warm smile and bowed.

"Ladies ..."

"Trevor, may I introduce you to Miss Elizabeth Bennet. Miss Elizabeth, may I present this handsome creature, my brother, Lord Latham."

Lord Latham reached for Elizabeth's hand and bestowed a light kiss. "I am honoured to meet you."

Elizabeth curtsied. "The pleasure is mine, your lordship."

Mere moments into pleasant conversation, Lord Latham's eyes drifted across the room. Both Elizabeth and Lady Gwendolyn immediately discerned the object of his distraction—the breath-taking Juliette, Duchess of Sexton. Lady Susan had pointed her out to Elizabeth soon upon their arrival that evening. No wonder he was distracted. Her striking green eyes were far lovelier than any emerald being worn in the ballroom. Lady Gwendolen looked as though she did not approve of Her Grace, leaving Elizabeth to wonder what in the two young women's history would engender such a fretful change in demeanour in her ladyship.

"Miss Bennet, again, it has been a pleasure meeting you. I shall look forward to the next time we meet." Lord Latham placed his hand upon his sister's arm. "Pardon me, dearest."

Casting her obvious disapproval of her brother's abrupt abandonment aside, her ladyship returned her attention to her companion. "Shall we return to the ballroom, Miss Elizabeth? My next set is promised to Lord Montclaire." She grimaced.

"You make it sound frightful."

"You have yet to meet Lord Montclaire. However, do not fret. I shall introduce you, and you may judge for yourself. Are you promised for the next set?"

"Indeed ... to a Sir Robert Boxley. Are you acquainted

with the gentleman?" Lady Susan had arranged everything.

"Indeed. You are in for similar excitement, I dare say." The two young ladies shared a knowing laugh and returned arm in arm to the ballroom with the familiarity of old acquaintances.

ೞೞೞ

The Season thus far had offered one succession of unsatisfying occasions after the other for Lady Gwendolen, as she was given to remind her brother, repining how weeks had passed, yet she had made no inroads with the elusive Mr. Darcy for he rarely attended social functions.

She walked into her brother's study and sat in one of the handsome leather chairs in front of his desk, lightly tapping her fingers until he gave her his full attention.

He looked up from his papers with concern. "Tell me what worries you now, dearest."

"Trevor, have you spoken with Mr. Darcy of late? Is he even in town?"

"Of course, he is in town. I see him often enough at my club. Why do you ask?"

"Oh, Trevor, why do you tease me so? You know that I am interested in seeing Mr. Darcy, in spending time in his company. Yet, I have not had the good fortune of doing so."

"Then we must rectify that situation. I am sure you have something in mind."

"Yes, I do. I was thinking of having an outing at the country estate in a week or so. That way, I will be sure to have Mr. Darcy's undivided attention."

He had hoped she would suggest such a scheme, for reasons he was not apt to divulge. He missed the Duchess's company. He especially missed the intimacy with her best afforded in the privacy of his country home. She had not made their being together easy of late.

He was not inclined to argue with his sister, even though

he had his doubts regarding her notion of having Darcy's undivided attention. "What makes you think Darcy will attend?"

"Why would he not? You only need to ask."

Lord Latham reflected on how Darcy had seemed unusually reclusive over the past weeks. He was no stranger to Darcy's proclivity to avoid social outings. This season, his friend seemed bent upon making it an art form.

"I shall do my best, though I offer no promises in that regard. Of course, the invitations must be extended to our usual guests, and I shall expect you to take care of that."

By now, his sister understood the unspoken meaning of his edict; the Duchess's name would grace the guest list. Lady Gwendolen had tried in the past to introduce her brother to eligible women of her acquaintance but it had been all for naught. He had already made his choice. He simply needed to go about the business of winning his ladylove over to his way of thinking. Lord Latham wished his sister would at least try to understand.

Chapter 7

What a glaring contrast between the haughty gentleman she had first met at the assembly in Meryton and the agreeable man who graced the ballroom that evening. She watched him dance with more than one young woman, obviously those with whom he was particularly acquainted, if his countenance was any indication. She watched him accept introductions to several others and noted that he spoke regularly to those around him.

Mr. Wickham said he was different amongst those who are his equal in consequence. This proves it.

Their eyes met. He nodded in acknowledgement of her presence. Elizabeth tore her eyes away. She hated being caught staring at *him,* of all people. Yet her eyes returned to the place wherever he happened to be standing, time and again. Oddly enough, she always found *him* looking back at her. She attributed her distraction to her present company, Sir Robert Boxley.

Sir Boxley, a plain looking man of six and twenty, had rightly discerned the object of Elizabeth's distraction to be none other than Fitzwilliam Darcy, as evident when he rolled his eyes. He leaned closer to her. "Miss Elizabeth, I trust you are not one of those women whose greatest ambition in life is to be the next mistress of Pemberley."

Elizabeth looked at him in puzzlement. "Certainly not! Why would you suggest such a thing?"

"Oh, never mind. I am glad to hear it, because that would be a foolish notion, I assure you. Men like him do not cavort with people like us."

He attempted to change the subject. "May I get you another drink?"

She looked at her glass, half-empty. "No, sir, I am satisfied with the one I have." She took a light sip for good measure. "Thank you for offering."

Elizabeth was often in the company of Sir Robert Boxley of late. This made Lady Susan happy. Elizabeth went along with the scheme, especially since it meant her ladyship did not try as hard to match her with someone else. At least he was amiable, but that was just it—he was just amiable. She had her own notion of what an ideal suitor ought to be. Of course, he must be a good man, respectable and forthright, but he also must challenge her, excite her, and render her unable to stop thinking of him. Elizabeth rarely thought of her current companion at all, unless he was standing next to her. Elizabeth surmised there were more pressing matters to which she must attend during her stay in town.

Perhaps once I have spoken with Mr. Bingley, and done what I might to reunite him with my sister, there will be time enough to fret over my own love life.

Elizabeth observed Mr. Darcy escape the crowded room through the balcony doors. *Now is the perfect time to speak with him.* "Excuse me, Sir Boxley. I am in need of a breath of fresh air."

"Certainly, Miss Elizabeth, I shall join you."

"No—no, it is not necessary. I shall be no more than a few minutes."

By the time of her arrival on the balcony, Elizabeth was surprised to find that there were several couples scattered about in intimate conversation. Panic reared its head, causing her heart to miss a beat. What would she do if she found Mr. Darcy similarly engaged? She wondered why she cared.

Luckily, she found him standing alone with his face turned heavenly, as if studying the night's sky. She quietly approached him from behind. She cleared her throat, garnering his attention. He turned to face her. His charming smile caught her quite off guard.

"Good evening, Mr. Darcy." Elizabeth found herself to be unequal to his penetrating stare. This was the first time they found themselves face to face since— She summoned her courage. She smiled, and she remembered to curtsey.

"Good evening, Miss Elizabeth. I noticed you earlier. I am surprised to see you here."

"I am here as a guest of Lady Susan's—Lady Susan Townes."

Darcy said nothing, sweeping his gaze over her intently, as if seeing ... every inch of her.

Not sure what to make of his demeanour, Elizabeth blushed, nearly forgetting her purpose in seeking him out in such a questionable manner with no regard for decorum. "Pray tell, Mr. Darcy, is Mr. Bingley coming here this evening, as well?"

"Though it is true that Bingley is one of my closest friends, I am not his keeper."

Now *there* was the haughty gentleman of her acquaintance. "Have you seen him recently?"

"Yes. I often see Bingley, a consequence of our being friends."

Was he taunting her? "Have you spoken to him about my being here in town?"

"Bingley knows that you are here in London, Miss Elizabeth."

"And have you told him what I asked of you as regards my sister Jane?"

"I said that I would not discuss such matters with Bingley, did I not?"

"Did he ask about my sister, Mr. Darcy?"

"Yes, he did ask about her. He wanted to know whether she, too, was in town."

"And what did you say?"

"I told him that she was not in town. Was I mistaken? Has your sister since ventured to town, as well?"

Elizabeth crossed her arms in front of her chest. "Certainly not!" She lowered her voice and continued, "As I informed you, Jane is quite devastated by Mr. Bingley's hasty leave taking. She is hardly in any state to travel to town. She is quite broken-hearted."

Darcy released an exasperated sigh. "I am sure she will accept matters for what they are, soon enough."

Elizabeth took a deep breath, and then held it a moment. *Why is he purposely baiting me?*

He must have surmised that she had reached the end of her patience with his teasing by the invisible arrows she shot from her eyes.

"Let us not argue, Miss Elizabeth. Tell me, how are you? Have you enjoyed your stay in town? Are you finding the Season diverting?"

"Yes, Mr. Darcy, I admit I am enjoying everything quite a bit, although you and I both know that is not why I am here. I am hoping for a chance to see Mr. Bingley."

"You might not expect to find him here tonight. He and I met earlier this evening, at another soirée."

Elizabeth did not try to hide her disappointment. "That is indeed unfortunate."

"Indeed."

Is he taunting me again? Can he not see how much this means to me? Elizabeth decided she had wasted enough of her evening with him. "Well, if you will pardon me, Mr. Darcy. I must return to the ballroom."

Darcy reached out to her, stopping short of touching her. "Must you return this instant?"

"Mr. Darcy, as you are always eager to point out to me, our being alone like this is hardly proper."

"That did not stop you from seeking me out." He raised his brow pointedly.

Elizabeth caught her breath. She fought the urge to protest.

"I meant to say, you are here, and it has been too long since—" His voice trailed off but his eyes spoke their own tale.

Since our last evening together in your home, she thought but did not dare utter aloud as she felt the colour wash over her entire body. Her mind filled with questions, but her heart whispered danger.

The sound of the orchestra getting ready for the next set recalled her to her purpose. "I must return. I will soon be missed."

"May I have a set with you this evening, Miss Elizabeth?"

"Mr. Darcy, I can honestly say that it does not disappoint me that my dance card is full. Good evening, sir."

೮೮೮೮

Lord Latham and Darcy sat at their usual table at White's, enjoying a round of drinks. The former had completed his agreement to do his sister's bidding by asking Darcy to join them at their upcoming party.

"What is this about? Why would Lady Gwendolen wish for a country party during this time of the Season?"

"My sister's motives are clear as regards you. I fear her

matchmaking plans now extend to my love life, as well. She is eager to have me get better acquainted with her new friend, though she will not admit it."

"I hesitate to go along with this scheme. Besides, I am expected at Rosings Park soon to visit Lady Catherine. Your invitation cuts into the time I plan to spend there."

"And we both know how excited you are over the prospect of going to Kent."

Darcy's quandary entailed more than that, a fact Lord Latham well understood. Though Darcy visited his aunt more out of a sense of responsibility than any sort of pleasure, he was proud to do it. Family meant everything to Darcy.

Lord Latham decided to sweeten the pot. "Look, if it makes a difference, I shall invite Lady de Bourgh and your cousin Anne, as well."

Darcy thought that was carrying things a bit far. "Why is this party necessary?"

"Gwendolen wants this. As you know I would do anything in my power to please her … including putting pressure on my friends."

"I am inclined to decline your invitation, if for no other reason than that."

"Ah! Nevertheless, you will not. If for nothing other than my sake, you will agree. Besides, there are advantages, as well, in that you will be excused from spending as much time in the company of yet another prospective bride in waiting."

"I surmise you are speaking of my cousin Anne. I hope that after all these years, she and Lady Catherine have abandoned that ridiculous notion."

After taking a huge swallow of his drink, Lord Latham began tapping the side of his glass with his long fingers. "For heaven's sake, agree already. What is keeping you in town?"

"If it means that much to you, I will come. And do not invite my aunt. I will explain things to her. Being a few days late should not raise her ire, especially if I extend my stay on the back end."

"Capital!"

"I have one condition."

"What is that?"

"You must agree to invite Charles Bingley."

"Bingley? Why Bingley?"

"I have my reasons."

"From our days at Cambridge to this day, I have never understood what you see in him? Or are you grooming him to be a suitable prospect for *your* sister?"

Even if that were the case, Darcy would be hard-pressed to come right out and confess it. He had spoken of the unfortunate events of Ramsgate with no one other than his cousin, a Colonel Fitzwilliam—Georgiana's other guardian.

In response to Lord Latham's taunt, Darcy said, "Bingley possesses the one trait in abundance which you, my friend, woefully lack."

"That being?"

"Subtlety."

Lord Latham laughed aloud. "That is not subtlety. I say the man is no fool. Why would he try to push his sister off on you? By contrast, Lady Gwendolen, you must admit, would be an excellent mistress of Pemberley."

"Do not fret, Trevor. Trust me, should my regard for your sister blossom into something more, and should I decide to act upon it, you will be the first to know."

"Other than the lady herself, I suspect." He raised an inquisitive brow in expectation of a fitting response.

Darcy smiled and raised his glass in jest. Lord Latham stood from his chair, announcing his intention to leave, but Darcy remained seated. He had much to contemplate. He signalled the waiter for another drink.

His friend was right in several respects. Lady Gwendolyn

was everything that a woman ought to be—everything the next mistress of Pemberley ought to be. Charming, intelligent, strikingly elegant. Indeed, she was everything ... except the woman he loved.

His fingers danced along the rim of his glass. It mattered not that he loved Elizabeth. Unbeknownst to her, she had bewitched him. All his unfailing efforts to ignore her presence in town nearly wiped away in one night. He knew she would be at the ball that evening. Her presence had been the single reason for his being there. Who knows what he might have done had that nondescript gentleman not attended her like a hawk?

Far better that he had maintained his reserve with her. Their worlds were not meant to coincide. Still, he needed to marry, he needed to beget the heir to Pemberley, and there was not much need in putting it off any longer. And his cousin Anne would never do.

Lady Gwendolen, on the other hand, try as he might to discourage her, seemed as determined as ever that she would have him. True, he was not in love with her, not yet. However, he was attracted to her. He considered it a good start. Perhaps after the upcoming party, it might be more.

Darcy finished his drink and then stood to take his leave with his mind made up. He owed it to himself; he owed it to his family, to try.

ಙಲಲಙ

Lady Gwendolen and Elizabeth sat in her ladyship's private sitting room, waiting to resume their conversation once the footman had gone. The two ladies increasingly spent regular time in each other's company. Elizabeth had even enquired of Lady Gwendolen's having an acquaintance with Mr. Bingley, on an earlier occasion.

"My brother says your Mr. Bingley has been invited to our country party, if that is any inducement in your accepting my invitation?"

"I assure you, he is not *my* Mr. Bingley." Elizabeth was quick to set the record straight on that point. "Who else is invited?"

"A number of others are expected, though you unlikely know any of them. Other than Mr. Bingley, whom I have yet to meet, the usual friends and acquaintances will be there. Please say you accept my invitation."

The fact that Elizabeth knew, perhaps, even fancied this Mr. Bingley did not dissuade her ladyship's purposes in inviting her a bit. Mr. Bingley, whoever he might be, was hardly competition for the earl. *Besides, my brother could stand such an impetus to spur him into action. He is fiercely competitive when it comes to that sort of thing.*

In addition, Lady Gwendolen had grown fond of Elizabeth even with their short acquaintance. Whilst others had taken issue with the fact of Elizabeth's having relatives in trade, Lady Gwendolen had been a staunch defender of her new friend. She was a gentleman's daughter, as well as connected to her own family by way of Lady Susan, who was connected to her aunt, Lady Langley—close enough in Lady Gwendolen's opinion.

Lord Latham returned to his home in time to find his sister and Elizabeth having tea. He darted his head inside the doorway, hoping for a quick courteous greeting that he might retire to his own affairs.

"Trevor! I did not expect you back this soon. You do remember my dear friend Miss Elizabeth?"

"Yes, I do. What a pleasure it is to see you again, Miss Elizabeth Bennet." He bowed slightly whilst retaining the position he had staked out in the doorway.

Lady Gwendolen placed her cup on the table, crossed the room, linked arms with his lordship, and cajoled him into the room. She led him to an empty spot next to Elizabeth. "Will you join us for tea?"

"I suppose I must." He looked at Elizabeth and smiled. "Are you enjoying the Season, Miss Elizabeth Bennet?"

Gwendolen handed her brother a cup. "Must there be such formality, Trevor? Are we not all friends? Surely, *Miss Elizabeth* is a fitting appellation."

"Your ladyship, I believe that is the lady's decision." Lord Latham graced Elizabeth with a mischievous smile. "How shall I address you, *my friend?*"

Lady Gwendolen, though pleased with the flirtatious tone, raised an inquisitive eyebrow.

"Miss Elizabeth, my lord. It pleases your sister. It pleases me, as well."

"Miss Elizabeth," he repeated, whilst holding Elizabeth's stare. He glanced at his sister for a second, "You are correct, *Miss Elizabeth* is much more fitting."

Smiling, Gwendolen approved of the budding attraction. "I have news. Miss Elizabeth has accepted our invitation to the country."

"Lady Gwendolen," Elizabeth said, "you know I have done no such thing. I must first speak with Lady Susan."

"Then it is settled, for Lady Susan has agreed to join us, as well." Lady Gwendolen smiled. "This will be a grand occasion for us all, will it not?"

Lord Latham and Elizabeth exchanged long glances. Lady Gwendolen dared not say anything to interrupt their silent discussion.

Will it not, indeed?

ಜಿಜಿಜಿ

Caroline barged through the doorway and demanded her say. "Charles, is it true that you are going to Lord Latham's country party?"

"Were you listening in on our conversation, Caroline?"

"Indeed, I was. How else am I to find out what you are

planning?" Caroline looked enraged. "How were you invited to Lord Latham's country estate, yet I was not? In light of that, how can you even consider his invitation?"

"You can hardly expect me to deny his lordship's request once he has deigned to bestow it!"

"What about me? I have yet to receive a request. Lord Latham and his sister have slighted our family in not inviting me."

"Leave it, Caroline. You do not know either of them! Why would they invite you to their home for a week?"

"Did they not invite you? Why on earth do you suppose they would do such a thing?"

Darcy grew tired of Caroline's tirade. Indeed, theirs was a love-hate relationship, if ever there were such a thing. She obviously loved pretending that he did not hate her, and he loved pretending that he did. "Miss Bingley, allow me to solve the mystery. Lord Latham invited Charles because I asked him to." He stood from his chair. "And before you ask, no, I will not impose upon Lord Latham's hospitality by suggesting he invite you as well."

Darcy turned his attention to Bingley. "I shall see you at White's tomorrow. Good night."

කරුණා

Elizabeth suspected Lady Gwendolen of playing matchmaker. She did not mind. The prospect of becoming better acquainted with his lordship intrigued her.

Almost done with her packing for the trip to Latham Hall, Elizabeth perused her latest letter from her sister Mary one more time, jumping right to the parts that interested her the most.

... Miss King is gone down to her uncle in Liverpool. She is gone to stay. Lydia asserts that Mr. Wickham is safe. He now spends more time than ever in the comfort of Longbourn. Lydia's behaviour is

*even more unguarded than before, and my words of admonishment to
our father remain unheeded, for he and Mama believe Mr. Wickham
to be the best of men. I suppose I have seen no evidence he is not,
though I cannot help but wonder about Miss King's uncle's decision
to send for her, thereby removing her from our environs in such a
precipitous manner.*

Elizabeth sighed. *Poor Mr. Wickham.* She skimmed the pages
for other happenings and settled once again on words of Jane's
situation.

*... Our dearest Jane says she is quite over Mr. Bingley, but I
prefer to think otherwise. By her actions, she fares no better, leaving
me to wonder at the veracity of our mother's sentiments. Might one
die of a broken heart? Please send word of your success as regards
Mr. Bingley.*

Your loving sister,
Mary

Elizabeth folded the letter and placed it inside the bundle
of letters she had received from the rest of her family since
she had arrived in town. Letters from everyone save Jane.

"Everything will be resolved before much longer, dearest
Jane," Elizabeth said aloud. "For the first time in weeks, I
shall have an audience with Mr. Bingley, finally giving birth to
truth and righting this horrible injustice. How happy you shall
be.

"Soon."

Chapter 8

Darcy and Lord Latham rode along slowly, allowing their prized steeds to recover after a hard, fast stint, moments earlier. Darcy had arrived late after the other guests had retired the evening before. Lord Latham and he had drinks and soon parted with plans for an early-morning ride. His late arrival had been a cause for concern for Lady Gwendolen, and she had insisted that her brother find out what his intentions were. Lord Latham had grown weary of trying to ascertain his friend's sentiments, but as Darcy had never rejected the notion of a possible alliance with her ladyship outright, he thought he might as well be done with the matter. The sooner the two had the requisite talk, the better.

"You must know that the purpose of this country soiree is to bring you one step closer to declaring yourself to Gwendolen."

Darcy cast Lord Latham a not-that-again warning glance. The two gentlemen had forged their bonds of friendship over the years, and had even enjoyed a private joke as regarded their kinship; Lord Latham may have enjoyed the title, but

71

Darcy enjoyed the fortune inherent in being the heir to Pemberley. While aristocracy aspired to power, financial fortune equalled power. He had always been there for Darcy when his father's favourite godson, George Wickham, had been too much to bear. On more than one occasion, Darcy went to Lord Latham's family estate on holidays, in lieu of Pemberley, to spare himself the grief of seeing Wickham ingratiate himself into the elder Mr. Darcy's good graces. Lord Latham was certain that either would do most anything for the other.

Reading his friend's wary expression, he silently apologised. "You know how this is with Gwendolen. I must have something to report to her."

"Then, shall we consider that you have honoured your obligation towards your sister."

"For now. You are not alone in my sister's schemes. As I told you, she is bent upon making a match for me, as well."

"Pray tell, which charming young debutante does she have in mind?"

"I am fairly certain you do not know the young lady. I barely know her, myself. I have met her only once, twice if you count my brief introduction to her at the Langley ball. If my sister has her say, I suppose that will change this week. I do not imagine I will be able to put if off any longer." Lord Latham considered the task ahead. He smiled.

"She is lovely. In fact, she is rather fascinating. I shall not consider it such a burden. However, from what I can tell she is not the type of woman whom I might seek as the next mistress of Latham Hall."

"How can you be certain? You admit to knowing little about her."

"My heart answers to another. I dare say she is not the type of woman who would turn a blind eye to my relationship with the exquisite Juliette, and I doubt I shall ever give her up … willingly."

As per his wont whenever the lovely widow's name was introduced into their conversations, Darcy held his tongue.

"I am well aware you do not approve of my relationship with Juliette."

"I imagine the heart wants what it wants," Darcy said. Lord Latham was stunned by his friend's remark. Darcy had been there during his darkest moment. He had seen what losing her to an older, richer, more powerful man nearly four years ago had done to him, how it had changed him. In vain, Darcy had tried to encourage him to move on, to accept what would never be, to forget her. The elder nobleman had since passed away. This was the first indication in years that Darcy's grievances against the Duchess were subsiding.

"Indeed, my heart yearns for Juliette. I am happy you understand. Mind if I ask when you became broadminded in that regard?"

Ignoring the question, Darcy said, "Does this rather sensible young woman have a name?"

"Yes. Miss Elizabeth Bennet—"

"Miss Elizabeth Bennet—"

"Look! My sister and Miss Elizabeth are just up the lane. Shall we join them?" Lord Latham raced ahead before Darcy could protest.

The first to arrive, Lord Latham jumped down from his horse and greeted them. "Good morning, ladies. What a pleasant surprise this is."

He could not help noticing how Elizabeth's smile froze in place with the arrival of the second horseman. His friend climbed down from his stallion and approached the party. Her eyes rested upon Darcy's eyes. His eyes fixed upon Elizabeth's. Lady Gwendolen's fixed upon Elizabeth's, as well.

"Mr. Darcy! What are you doing here?"

"Miss Elizabeth," Darcy said whilst bowing. "I am Lord Latham's guest."

Their eyes posed the questions their lips would not. Lord Latham felt as if he and his sister were intruding upon a private moment.

"Do you know Mr. Darcy?"

Given her silence, he wondered if she had heard his sister's question.

"Yes, Lady Gwendolen ... a little. We met in Hertfordshire." She seemed uneasy.

Lord Latham looked at his friend for some sort of explanation. Never had he observed Darcy behold another woman as he beheld Elizabeth.

"Ladies, may we escort you to the house? My friend and I are famished. Perhaps you will join us for breakfast."

Darcy extended his arm to Elizabeth. Lord Latham read the schooled response on his sister's face to his friend's neglect as she moved quickly to accept his proffered arm, as though he meant it for her. "We shall be delighted to have breakfast with you." She turned towards Elizabeth. "Will we not, Miss Elizabeth?"

"Indeed," Elizabeth said rather tentatively

Lord Latham offered his arm to Elizabeth, and she graciously accepted. The two couples preceded side by side, his lordship wondering at his friend's preference for one woman over the other.

ೠೠೠ

Later, Lady Gwendolen found him alone in his study managing last-minute estate business before attending to his other, far more pressing duties as lord of the manor house.

"Trevor, did you know that Mr. Darcy and Miss Elizabeth had a prior acquaintance?"

"I was as surprised as you, dearest."

"I hope this does not interfere with my plans."

"Plans?"

"How many times must I remind you of my wish for Miss Elizabeth and you to become better acquainted during her stay? I expect you to use every opportunity to your advantage in that regard."

"I will do what I can, for your sake. However, I make no promises, dearest, for I am more than capable of choosing my own wife."

"Trevor, I have bad news, I am afraid. The Duchess's arrival is delayed."

He looked up from his papers. "Delayed? Why have I heard nothing of this before now?"

"I only received word before coming to see you." She handed him the express. He took it and perused its contents. It displeased him.

His sister reached out to retrieve the letter he had tossed aside. "I dare say it is not the end of the world. A day or two delays her. She is not the only guest to be detained you know. The weather is not cooperating with my plans for the week."

"Somehow, you do not sound disappointed."

Gwendolen walked behind the desk and wrapped her arm about his shoulders. "Indeed, I am not; nor should this turn of events dishearten you. As long as each of our guests arrives safely, I shall not complain. In the meantime, we shall see that those who have arrived already are pleasantly engaged at all times."

"I believe I can take a hint, dearest. Now, run along. I have matters to resolve before this evening's festivities."

After his sister quit the room, Lord Latham leaned back in his chair and pressed his hands along his temple. Reflecting on his last meeting with the Duchess, he supposed he might have pushed her too far in demanding that she accept his proposal of marriage. He sat straight in his chair and reached for a quill and paper. He composed a letter to her, declaring therein his resignation to the fact that what he wanted most would never be. Thus, his greatest wish was that they would remain as they ever were. He closed his ardent missive with the following words:

... Tarry in town no longer, my heart, for I am aching with the need to express the depths of my affection for you upon your safe arrival.

🙠🙣🙠🙣

Darcy recalled how he had tried his best to mask his disappointment in having the wrong woman on his arm earlier that day. Except, she was not the wrong woman, was she? Had he not decided that he would take advantage of their time in the country to woo her ladyship, to see where it might lead? Had all his plans fled in the face of his heart's true desire?

Upon spending time in the company of both Elizabeth and Lady Gwendolen for most of the morning, Darcy decided that the current week was not the time to act upon his plan. He simply enjoyed Elizabeth's company too much to expend the energy it would take to distract himself from her long enough to woo Lady Gwendolen properly. Besides, Darcy was not pleased with the prospect of his friend being better acquainted with Elizabeth. Although a future between them was impossible, given the inferiority of her circumstances, he cared for her too much to stand by and allow what his friend probably had in mind. Darcy stewed as he observed Lord Latham speaking intimately with Elizabeth across the room, whilst he remained ensnared in lacklustre conversation with another guest, discussing politics, of all things.

Having fulfilled his obligation to Lady Gwendolen for the evening, speaking with her long enough to satisfy her expectations but not too much as to excite her hopes, Darcy wanted only to trade places with Lord Latham——to bathe in Elizabeth's warm smiles and what he was certain was witty repartee.

"I concede to your greater wisdom," Darcy said to his

aristocratic companion the first chance he could. He placed his empty glass on the tray of a passing footman and strolled across the room.

"May I join you two?"

"As a matter of fact—"

Elizabeth interrupted his lordship's rebuff. "You are more than welcome to join us, Mr. Darcy. Lord Latham and I are discussing Sir John Keats. I believe you were about to recite his latest piece, were you not, my lord?"

Darcy cast his friend a knowing smile. "Somehow, I am not surprised. My friend has a penchant for spewing poetry to those with the fortitude to bear it."

"Forgive me, my friend, if I cannot help but share my passion for fine sonnets, especially in the presence of such beauty."

Such flattery flowing from Lord Latham's lips was but one factor in Elizabeth's ready acquiescence to Mr. Darcy's joining them. Lord Latham was everything a gentleman ought to be, his good looks exceeded only by his charms. Elizabeth suspected he was used to having his way.

She graced Darcy with a tantalising smile. "I am reminded of my initial meeting with Mr. Darcy, where there was a similar mention of poetry being the food of love."

"Yes, and if I recall correctly, you declared it the surest way of starving any fragile regard. In fact, I believe you offered the perfect remedy for encouraging affection."

"Not that it affected you."

"Excuse me, you two, I insist upon having my share of the conversation."

"Of course, your lordship. I first met Mr. Darcy at an assembly where he danced with no one except the members of his own party."

"Somehow, I do not find that surprising, knowing him as I do."

"You may also recall that I have since taken advantage of every opportunity to make amends for our first meeting, have I not, Miss Elizabeth?"

A slight commotion on the other side of the room drew Lord Latham's attention. "If you two will excuse me, this matter warrants my involvement." He stepped away slowly and then paused to look back. "I hesitate to leave you alone with this gentleman."

"Take your time. Miss Elizabeth is in good hands, I assure you."

Lord Latham walked away, looking back once again in wonderment.

"Do you and your friend often speak to each other so, Mr. Darcy? Whatever does he mean in saying he hesitates to leave the two of us alone?"

"I am sure I do not know what he meant."

Elizabeth harrumphed. "I am rather sure you do. I begin to ask myself which of the two of you is the most charming."

"Are you laughing at me, Miss Elizabeth?"

"Heaven forbid."

"Then might I assume you are flirting with me?"

"Assume what you like."

"I assume you are. In fairness to you, I must tell you that no benefit will result."

"Whatever do you mean, sir?"

"I am no more inclined to interfere in Bingley's situation now than when you first asked."

"I believe you would interfere soon enough if you thought it were in your own interest."

"What are you insinuating?"

"Having met Miss Darcy, I can honestly say she has no interest in Mr. Bingley. However, I begin to suspect that Miss Caroline Bingley is not the only one who desires an alliance between your families where your sister and Mr. Bingley are concerned."

"You could not be further from the truth."

"Prove it, Mr. Darcy. Speak with Mr. Bingley on my sister's behalf."

"I will do even better. Bingley will arrive here tomorrow. You may speak with him yourself."

"Yes, Lady Gwendolen has assured me that Mr. Bingley will be joining us for the week. If nothing else, I ask that you do nothing to impede my ability to speak with him."

"You have my word, Miss Elizabeth." He smiled. "Now, shall we call a truce?"

Elizabeth conceded. Mr. Darcy need not be her enemy. He raised her proffered hand to his lips.

"Yes, Mr. Darcy. Let us consider our differences a thing of the past."

છાછાછા

What Lady Gwendolen observed of Mr. Darcy's behaviour that evening displeased her. Not only had he contrived to escort Elizabeth to dinner, the two had sat together. She planned to speak with the butler. From that night on, formal seating assignments would be the rule.

Whilst she could not complain about the amount of Mr. Darcy's attention she had garnered, for he had spent more time attending her that evening than ever before, throughout the entire time she could tell his true focus was her brother and Elizabeth. *He behaved as though he were jealous.*

Sally tucked the remaining locks behind her ladyship's ears and finished braiding her hair. She stepped back and admired her work.

"That should do it, your ladyship." Despite being her lady's maid, Sally and she enjoyed a close camaraderie, made even stronger since the loss of her ladyship's parents.

"How did you enjoy the company of the gentleman from

Derbyshire, my lady? I am sure he fought hard to tear his eyes away from you all evening."

Gwendolen stood, placed her hand on her waistline, and studied her image.

"Is there something amiss, your ladyship?"

"Sally, I need your help."

"Anything for you, your ladyship. How might I serve you?"

"What I ask of you is a matter of some delicacy. However, my curiosity demands satisfaction."

Gwendolen walked across the room and sat on her bed. "I have reason to suspect that my friend, Miss Elizabeth, is more acquainted with Mr. Darcy than she will allow. Ask around and find out what you can. If she is my competition for Mr. Darcy's affection, I must know."

"I understand, your ladyship. Give me leave, and I shall make inquiries amongst acquaintances in town."

"Please, do what you must. I caution you, however, to be discrete."

છાજીભ

Lady Gwendolen drew herself away from the window of her brother's study. The steady pounding of rain that had started the evening before was sure to delay the arrival of the last of the guests, if they even still were decided to attend. She took comfort in knowing that her particular guests were already in residence. Those delayed included the Duchess and Mr. Bingley, and since both had been invited at her brother's request, she did not intend to make herself too upset by their absence.

As for the former, the Duchess, Lady Gwendolen should have been pleased by the delay, except that it had made no difference.

"Trevor, how goes your quest to become acquainted with Miss Elizabeth?"

"Your quest for me to become better acquainted with Miss Elizabeth is progressing nicely."

"She is charming."

Lord Latham nodded at the appropriate time. Lady Gwendolen supposed that Her Grace's absence occupied his thoughts. He had that look.

"Mr. Darcy seems of that opinion."

Lord Latham said nothing.

"I hate it when you ignore me."

"I beg your pardon, dearest?" His brows were drawn together, as if his mind raced to determine what he had missed of their discussion.

"Did you not notice how Mr. Darcy attended Miss Elizabeth last evening?"

"Having learned of their prior acquaintance, I would not expect him to do otherwise." He looked into her eyes. "Is that what is bothering you? He was only being considerate, I assure you, what with Miss Elizabeth's being surrounded by strangers."

"Are you quite certain?"

"Yes, I am. For as long as I have known Darcy, he has never shown interest in a woman whose circumstances were decidedly beneath his own."

"That is a small consolation, I suppose. Still, I would rest easier if you spent more time entertaining Miss Elizabeth yourself. If I am to make any progress with Mr. Darcy this week, the last thing I need is competition."

"I promised that I would get to know Miss Elizabeth better, and I will. These things take time, and I am in no hurry."

Lady Gwendolen crossed her arms in protest, as she was wont to do whenever her brother did not give her opinions adequate consideration.

"Let us have none of that." Lord Latham strolled across

the room and offered his arm to his sister. "I know how much you wish to make a good impression on my friend this week, dearest. However, I caution you against being too zealous. We gentlemen rather enjoy the chase." He kissed her forehead. "Now, come let us join our guests for breakfast."

೮೦೮೦೮೦

By midday, all had congregated in the drawing room. Lady Susan and Lady Alexandria paired in a card game with Lord Langley and Sir Downing. Darcy, Lord Latham, Lady Gwendolen, and Elizabeth were likewise engaged in a lively game of cassino, and the rest of the guests took up books for their afternoon diversion.

"Please play something for us, Gwendolen," Lady Alexandria said.

Lord Langley seconded his wife's request. "Yes, please do. What would a rainy afternoon at Latham Hall be without your musical genius?"

Never one to disappoint, Lady Gwendolen, an accomplished musician, regaled her guests for nearly a half hour. When it was Elizabeth's turn to exhibit, she soon found Mr. Darcy rising from his chair with an offer to turn the pages for her.

"No, Mr. Darcy, I assure you that it is not necessary."

"I insist."

The two took their place at the instrument, and Elizabeth started looking through the music sheets.

"Mr. Darcy, if you mean to intimidate me by your presence, you need not bother. I am not ashamed to admit that my proficiency does not compare to Lady Gwendolen's or your sister's from what I have been told."

"I recall your exhibition in Meryton. I was delighted, as I am sure each one here will be."

"This is the finest instrument I have ever seen." Elizabeth touched the keys with a light brush of her fingertips. "Lady Gwendolen's performance was splendid." Elizabeth silently chastised herself for not having made better use of her time and practised more.

Darcy laid his hand on her fingers, calming her nervousness in one regard, but inciting her in another. "You will be fine, Miss Elizabeth. Why not begin with Beethoven's fifth. You performed the piece wonderfully when we were in Meryton."

She marvelled at how he had recalled her exhibition from so many months ago. Elizabeth smiled. Together, they located the sought-after music sheet, and Elizabeth began to play. She could easily discern his pleasure in her performance by their exchange of furtive glances. Elizabeth hoped no one else in the room noticed how he looked at her throughout the piece, especially Lady Gwendolen. She knew by now how much the gentleman meant to her ladyship. She did not mean for Lady Gwendolen to perceive her as any sort of rival for his affections ... even if he did stir her passions as no other man had ever done previously.

"Mr. Darcy, are you concerned about Mr. Bingley's delay in arriving?" Elizabeth said at the end.

"His delay is possibly attributable to his trying to dodge his sister Miss Bingley."

"You mean to say Miss Bingley is not invited?"

"No, she is not ... to her dismay."

"Why is that?"

"She has no prior acquaintance with Lord Latham or Lady Gwendolen; Bingley's acquaintance is fleeting, at best. He is coming because I asked Lord Latham to invite him."

"Why would you want to invite Mr. Bingley if they are not acquainted ... unless—" Elizabeth looked at Darcy pointedly. "Mr. Darcy, did you wish to have him here as a means of keeping us apart on the chance our paths might cross in town?"

His mouth falling open, Darcy feigned astonishment that she would suggest such a thing. "If that were my intention, I have failed miserably, have I not?"

"Have you? For all I know, you may have persuaded Mr. Bingley against coming once you discovered me here."

"How would I have done that?"

"I put little past a man of your means. You are no doubt used to arranging things for your own convenience."

"Then, why would I do such a thing? I promised I would not interfere in your quest to see Bingley. To do otherwise would mean an end to our truce, would it not?"

"I shall not argue your point, sir."

"Good, for I much prefer when you and I are not at odds."

"I tend to think otherwise, Mr. Darcy. Our history suggests you rather enjoy provoking me."

With a confident grin, Darcy acknowledged the veracity of her charge. "Perhaps, but I wager the joy I receive pales in comparison to the pleasure you get in rising to my every challenge."

Wide-eyed, Elizabeth was speechless.

The lull in music must have drawn the attentions of some of the others. Lord Latham joined Elizabeth and his friend at the instrument.

"The two of you seem to have lost the meaning of exhibiting. Darcy, you do not mind if I take your place at Miss Elizabeth's side, I am sure."

Darcy relinquished his seat to his lordship. "Certainly not. Pardon me, Miss Elizabeth. I shall look forward to continuing our debate."

Elizabeth smiled nervously and averted her eyes. Lord Latham looked at his friend, and then he looked at Elizabeth, his eyes silently questioning.

ೞೞೞೞ

Lady Gwendolen's maid had been one tireless truth ferret. The next morning found Sally in her ladyship's apartment earlier than had been her wont.

"Your ladyship, I have news."

"News?"

"Yes, my lady. It turns out your suspicions regarding Miss Elizabeth Bennet are not unfounded."

"What? I mean to say, how? I thought it might take days, weeks even."

"As did I, your ladyship. However, it turns out that my cousin, who now works downstairs in the kitchen, recently left Mr. Darcy's employment at his London home."

Lady Gwendolen sat upon her bed and folded her legs beneath her in anticipation. "Please, tell me everything. Do not keep me in suspense."

"First, I confess it took quite a bit of coaxing on my part to persuade my cousin where her loyalties now lie."

"Of course, I understand, and you need not tell me her name, if that is any assurance."

"I appreciate it, but I have no concerns in that regard. I assured my cousin she shall suffer no retribution."

"Excellent. What does your cousin say?"

"It turns out Miss Elizabeth Bennet spent an entire night with Mr. Darcy in his London home—only the two of them, save a few servants."

Aghast, Lady Gwendolen coloured. "I have befriended a … a fallen woman. No! This cannot be true."

"I am afraid it is true, my lady. My cousin carried this burden from the moment of Miss Elizabeth Bennet's arrival at Latham Hall the other day. You see, she recognised the young lady from having carried a tray up to her ... in the mistress's suite."

"I never would have expected to hear anything as scandalous as this. Please, tell no one else of what you heard."

"I assure you, I shall not repeat a word."

"Please, help me prepare for the day." Her ladyship climbed down from her huge poster bed and walked over to her dressing table. "I must speak with my brother. He will know what to do."

"Yes, your ladyship."

Sally was rather quiet as she carried out her morning routine. Her ladyship had not enquired on the details of her cousin's knowledge of her former employer's affairs and she was glad that she had not. The truth may have cast aspersions on her cousin's account, possibly resulting in her dismissal from her current position, were it made known that she had left Darcy House in disgrace, terminated for having spoken to other household staff not already privy to the information of Miss Elizabeth Bennet's being there. Without informing the master, the butler had taken it upon himself to send her on her way. In fact, Sally had been the means of securing her cousin's place in Latham Hall. She prayed she would not be the means of her removal. Lady Gwendolen promised that would not be the case. Sally took some comfort in that. She trusted her ladyship implicitly. Her promise was as good as gold.

Chapter 9

Lady Gwendolen walked back and forth across the floor of her brother's study, having confided in him everything she had heard some moments earlier from her lady's maid.

Tired of her pacing and having had time to take in the information, he stood from his desk, approached his sister, and embraced her.

The comfort of his arms let loose the tears she had fought desperately to hold back.

"Please, do not fret. This is not the end of the world. For all we know, it is untrue, mere rumour and unfounded speculation."

"How can we be certain? I have seen how he looks at her. Theirs is more than a mere acquaintance. She is his ... his mistress! How could she deceive me this way?"

"Let us not jump to conclusions. I am certain there is more to this than meets the eye. Besides, since seeing the two together, I have had time to consider something Darcy said to me when he visited us earlier this year. He congratulated himself on having saved a friend from an unfortunate alliance with a young woman from Hertfordshire owing to her low connections and her unsuitable family. I am certain he was speaking of his friend, Bingley, in light of the two of them having spent the past autumn together. Perhaps he prevented his friend from marrying Miss Elizabeth or one of her sisters."

"If what you say is true, and he merely sought to save his friend from an alliance with a family with no connections, it does not mean he would not seek such a woman as his mistress."

Lady Gwendolen wondered why her brother looked at her so, as if stunned by her declaration. Did he think she was naïve? She had witnessed the way Mr. Darcy looked at Elizabeth when he thought no one else was aware. She had witnessed the same gaze in her brother's eyes when he looked at the Duchess. Too many times to recount.

"A young woman's reputation is at stake. Darcy is a friend. I will not have a scandal on account of rumours circulated from this house. Say nothing of these unfounded allegations to anyone."

"Naturally, I shall not. I am fond of Miss Elizabeth. I have no desire to hurt her. Besides, how would that suit my purposes?"

"I believe you, dearest."

"But what if the rumours are more widely circulated than we know? What if Mr. Darcy should offer to marry Miss Elizabeth in hopes of quieting the speculations? He obviously holds her in some esteem." *How I wish he looked at me the way he looks at her.*

"We do not know the entire story. If it is true, he has not done anything yet. Maybe he will do nothing."

"What if his honour combined with the threat of scandal compels him to marry her?"

Lord Latham placed his hand upon his sister's. "He may

well marry her, but that would be his choice, would it not?"

Tears pooled in her eyes once more. "I cannot lose him ... not to a fallen woman ... not this way."

"Only he can decide how this matter will be handled. He is my friend. You do understand I will support him in whatever decision he makes."

She felt crushed by his avowal. He pulled her into his embrace again. "Fear not, dearest. I shall speak with Darcy."

After a few moments, Lady Gwendolen gained her composure. "Thank you, Trevor. I had better attend our guests."

"Good idea. I shall join you shortly." He walked across the room to ring the bell.

"What are you planning?"

"I am summoning Mr. Johnson to locate Darcy. I need to speak with my friend as soon as can be."

ଓଅଓ

Darcy and Elizabeth sat in the drawing room enjoying their tentative camaraderie born the evening before. She no longer faulted him if he happened to benefit from Caroline's scheme in separating her brother from Jane, nor the fact he had turned a blind eye. Besides, as Bingley's closest friend, she and Mr. Darcy would often be thrown in each other's company once the confusion was cleared away.

The door of the drawing room opened and in walked Mr. Bingley. His surprise in seeing Elizabeth was great indeed. Any anger she held against him pursuant to his abandonment of her sister fled in the face of the unaffected cordiality with which he expressed himself on seeing her again.

"Miss Elizabeth, I had no idea I might see you here this week. Darcy spoke of your being in town. You must tell me how you are enjoying your stay."

Elizabeth answered him in the usual way.

He sat in the seat next to her. "How is everyone in your

family?"

In Elizabeth's manner of thinking, Bingley's eyes asked the question he dare not voice aloud. He continued in a tone that engendered something akin to regret, "A long time has passed since I have had the pleasure of seeing you ... not since November, when we were all dancing together at Netherfield."

Elizabeth took it as a good sign. Anxious to ease the awkward tension, she opened her mouth to speak, but was forestalled.

Bingley asked nervously, "Are all your sisters at Longbourn, still?"

Bingley's face beamed pursuant to her affirmative response. Indeed, a good sign.

Once again, the doors were opened. Lady Gwendolen entered the room. Both gentlemen stood.

"Lady Gwendolen, may I introduce Mr. Bingley." Darcy said.

She smiled and offered Bingley her hand. "Welcome to Latham Hall, Mr. Bingley. Now that I have met you, I do recall seeing you in Mr. Darcy's company. However, I do not believe we were ever formally introduced."

"I am delighted finally to meet you, your ladyship. I am honoured to have been invited here this week."

"I do hope we shall become better acquainted during your stay." Lady Gwendolen turned to Elizabeth. "Miss Elizabeth, may I steal you away for a stroll in my gardens?"

"Pardon me. I was hoping to have a word with Mr. Bingley," Elizabeth said.

"You promised we would have a walk about the gardens. Besides, I want a moment alone with you before the others come down." Lady Gwendolen urged Elizabeth to stand and then linked arms with her, determined to have her way.

Kind and amiable, Bingley's face registered her ladyship's

resolve. "Yes, I shall go to my rooms to speak with my man. Shall I see you later this afternoon, Miss Elizabeth?"

"Indeed, Mr. Bingley, for I dearly wish to speak with you." Elizabeth looked at his friend to gauge his response and was pleased by what she saw.

Bingley blessed her with a most obliging smile. "I can hardly wait, Miss Elizabeth."

಄಄಄

The two young ladies walked arm in arm along the garden path. "Mr. Bingley is a pleasant gentleman. I am no longer surprised by your knowing Mr. Darcy with Mr. Bingley being such a great friend of his."

"Yes, Mr. Darcy is especially kind to Mr. Bingley. He seems more of a guardian of him than a friend."

"From what my brother told me this morning, Mr. Bingley is eminently indebted to Mr. Darcy. Of course, it is merely speculation on my part. I have no reason to suppose that Mr. Bingley was the person my brother meant when he said that Mr. Darcy had taken a great deal of pride in having saved a close friend from the misfortunes of a most imprudent marriage."

"What do you mean, your ladyship?"

"Mind you, my brother said nothing of the particulars, though I suspect the last thing Mr. Darcy would want is for the lady's family to learn of his involvement."

"I, for one, shall not mention it."

"I would appreciate it if you did not. Again, my brother mentioned none of the specifics; in fact, he told me what little he did as a means of reminding me of Mr. Darcy's loyalty and steadfastness as a true friend."

"Why would Mr. Darcy do such a thing?"

"According to my brother, Mr. Darcy found the young lady's family entirely unsuitable, vulgar, and quite objectionable." Insofar as Elizabeth's troubled countenance told her that she had hit her mark, Lady Gwendolen considered her mission accomplished.

"Good heavens! I did not mean for us to be away for so long. I must return before the other guests begin moving about."

"Lady Gwendolen, please do not think me rude. I am of a mind to enjoy a longer walk before returning to the house."

As the two commenced to head off in opposite directions, Lady Gwendolen said, "No—no, take as much time as you need."

శుభుభు

"Darcy, I am surprised you would stand by and allow my sister to befriend a woman whom you have compromised."

"Compromised? What are you saying?"

"Do you deny that you have compromised Miss Elizabeth Bennet? Most egregiously, I might add."

"I take offense to your accusing me thus. Miss Elizabeth Bennet is a gentlewoman. How dare you call into question her character by merely suggesting such a thing? You know me better than that."

"I thought I did. However, in light of what is being said about the two of you in some circles, I have to wonder."

"Whatever do you mean?"

"Rumour is of Miss Elizabeth having spent the night alone with you in your home. Is this true?"

Darcy stood and stormed about the room. Blood rushed to his head. He said nothing.

Lord Latham pounded his fist on the desk. "You mean to say these accusations are true!"

"No! Although it is true that Miss Elizabeth spent the night at my home, nothing untoward occurred. Miss Elizabeth called on me at Darcy House. She could have no way of knowing we would be alone."

"Then there is a misunderstanding? Not that it matters, as you well know. I wish to know for my own purposes."

"Actually, Miss Elizabeth fell extremely ill. I dared not do anything but care for her as best I could."

Lord Latham strode over to his liquor cabinet. "Thank you for clarifying the situation for me. I knew there had to have been a reasonable explanation."

"Yes, for what it is worth."

Having poured two drinks, he handed one to his friend. "Indeed, still this matter must be dealt with."

"You need not state what is obvious to me."

"What do you intend to do?"

Darcy's eyes veered towards the window. He espied Lady Gwendolen walking along the path towards the manor house, alone.

Darcy took one swallow and slammed his glass down on the table. "I know what I must do."

Chapter 10

Elizabeth walked about, her mind everywhere but her immediate surroundings. *All this time it was Mr. Darcy. Mr. Darcy, not Caroline Bingley. Oh, she probably had a hand in the scheme—but Mr. Darcy!*

As if intending to exasperate herself as much as possible against Mr. Darcy, she reminded herself of their last evening at Netherfield Park, what was without question the beginning of the end for her sister's hopes. She recalled how he had watched his friend attending her sister, with what she now recognised as disfavour. How he had mocked her every time they had seen each other since her arrival in town, even laughed whenever she mentioned Jane's heartbreak. How was she to remain in proximity to the man who had boasted shamelessly of the misery he had inflicted upon a most beloved sister?

Continuing along the path, she could not think of leaving the country without remembering her purpose in even being there in the first place. Although the prospect of knowing Lord Latham better had intrigued her, the opportunity to speak with

Mr. Bingley had been more compelling. As she considered Mr. Bingley, she had to wonder if one so easily swayed by the opinion of his friend to abandon the woman he loved could make her sister happy. Elizabeth had much to contemplate, and she determined to walk on to settle her mind on what to do as regarded her sister's fickle lover.

Any semblance of calm afforded her by the quiet serenity and the fresh awakenings of the early spring morning fled when, to her utter amazement, Mr. Darcy stood directly before her.

"Miss Elizabeth, I have purposely sought you out. I hope you do not mind. We must talk."

"I am afraid, Mr. Darcy, this is an inopportune moment. I must return to the house."

"I beg of you, please, listen to what I have to say."

Gone was the hint of goodwill engendered by their friendly banter the evening before, taking with it any desire for civility. "Can this not wait, Mr. Darcy?" She had not wished to be rude, regardless of how much he deserved it. What choice had she?

"What I am about to tell you will not be easy to hear, but hear it, you must." Despite Elizabeth's cold reception and apparent disinterest, he pressed on. "I wish to start by saying that you need not worry for I have the solution."

"This sounds ominous." Elizabeth met his awkward demeanour with wide-eyed curiosity. "Pray tell what this is about."

"I am afraid it has to do with the time we spent alone at my home some weeks ago. Others have learned of the incident—by a disgruntled servant, I suppose.

"Now, there is the threat of a scandal should the wrong people become privy to the information."

Elizabeth felt embarrassed as she considered that if what he was saying were true, she had no one but herself to blame. "You say you have a solution. What do you propose?"

"I propose we marry. Marry me, Miss Elizabeth, that I might protect you from this threat of scandal and ruination."

"You speak as though you are granting a favour, Mr. Darcy."

"If not for my love for you, then, yes, I would be granting you a favour. As I am in love with you, and have been for months, if I am to be honest, you need not consider it as such."

"You love me, Mr. Darcy?"

"Yes, although I have struggled in vain these past months that I would not act upon it. This incident has forced me to realise my feelings will not be repressed. I admire and love you, most ardently."

Elizabeth's bewilderment was beyond expression. She stared in disbelief yet kept silent.

"You are astonished by my declaration. Indeed, though no more astonished than I am in even suffering such feelings. Alas, I cannot command my heart for if I could exercise such control, I would not have subjected myself to the scorn, the derision, and the degradation that must surely come with such an unequal alliance as ours."

As if taking Elizabeth's silence as encouragement to push the merits of his proposal forth, Mr. Darcy pressed on. "Though I never wished to disappoint my family in this way, nor did I ever wish for a marriage borne out of necessity, the fact that I am in love with you, and my suspicions that you are not indifferent towards me, are a start, something we might build upon."

Darcy traced his fingers through his hair and looked away. "I have no other choice. I am honour bound to protect you, even if it means I must now congratulate myself on the hope of relations whose conditions in life are decidedly beneath my own."

He had said enough. The simmering rage inside Elizabeth boiled over. "You may not have a choice in this matter, Mr. Darcy, but I certainly do. I would sooner return to Longbourn and never show my face in polite society again than marry you."

Darcy's face manifested his awe! "What? What are you saying? Are you rejecting me?"

"You heard me correctly, Mr. Darcy."

"But why, and with no pretence of civility, I might add, when I have told you of my love for you?"

"What I heard you say is you would be marrying me against your better judgment, at the risk of disappointing your family. And why, Mr. Darcy—because of the threat of scandal?"

"Because I wish to protect your reputation. Because I do not wish to see you ruined. The fact that I am in love with you and have been for months makes the ensuing mortification bearable."

"Why must either of us suffer? What transpired at your home between the two of us that either of us must hang our heads in shame?"

"Even if the worst happened, I would suffer no disgrace as a result, and you would be wise to consider that, Miss Elizabeth." Her stubbornness unbridled his temper. "You arrived at my doorstep, unescorted. You fell ill. I merely did all that was necessary to protect you, then, as I am honour bound to do now."

"Perhaps you took unfair advantage of me, and that is why you believe you must protect me—to ease your guilty conscience."

"I did what I needed to do. My conscience is clear. However, others may misconstrue *your* motives in coming to my home in the first place."

He threw his hands up in frustration. "I fail to understand why we are arguing, and I mean to put an end to it. What is done is done, and now the knowledge or lack thereof is public. We must marry. You need to resolve yourself to that fact."

Darcy stepped closer and offered his hand to Elizabeth. She flinched and stepped away.

"Never! Do you think for one minute that any consideration, even the avoidance of scandal, would tempt me to accept the man who has been the means of ruining, perhaps forever, the happiness of my dearest sister?"

Elizabeth wanted to believe the man who stood before her had some semblance of humanity, compassion, dignity, a measure of regret. He had admitted being in love with her. Perhaps Lady Gwendolen had the account wrong. "Can you deny that you influenced Mr. Bingley to abandon Jane?"

Darcy said nothing, spurring Elizabeth on. "I no longer wonder why you refused my repeated pleas to right this injustice. All along, you have been its chief perpetrator."

"I have no wish of denying I did everything in my power to separate my friend from your sister. I detected no special regard from your sister towards Bingley. Certainly, she smiled whenever he spoke, quite obsessively to the point of being insincere. However, that alone did not sway me against her. You heard your mother speak of the *supposed* alliance during supper that evening at the Netherfield ball. She spoke in such terms of inevitability as to be taken as mercenary.

"You cannot deny it. Did you expect me to rejoice in such an unfortunate prospect for my friend?"

No, Elizabeth could not deny his assertion as she recalled the shame and embarrassment she suffered because of her mother's behaviour. Still, she did not intend to let him escape the burden of culpability as easily as that.

"My dislike of you is not founded merely on this matter. My opinion of you was decided long before I learned of your part in my sister's predicament. Your character was unfolded when Mr. Wickham gave me an account of your cruelty against him. What can you have to say in defence of your self-ishness towards him?"

"Why in heaven do you take such an eager interest in that gentleman's affairs?"

"Why would I not, knowing as I do of his misfortunes?"

"His misfortunes!" Darcy said with utter contempt. "Yes, he is the most unfortunate creature which ever slithered across the earth."

"You are to blame for his current state, yet you mock and ridicule him. Have you no shame, Mr. Darcy?"

"How dare you think so little of me?" He failed to conceal his anger, his disappointment. "I suppose in some twisted sort of way, I should be grateful. Knowing where I stand in your estimation serves us both well.

"It pains me to consider that you think highly of him and poorly of me. Nevertheless, it is beside the point. You and I must marry!"

Elizabeth's heartbeat thundered with rage. "Never! The next time you boast of the great satisfaction you enjoyed in saving your friend from the prospect of such inferior connections, boast of saving yourself, as well!

"For regardless of the words you speak of loving me, even against your reason, I am quite certain I do not love you. I despise you, not only for what you have done to my sister, but for as long as I have known you. Your arrogance, your conceit, and your selfish disdain of the feelings of others, I find deplorable.

"You, Mr. Darcy, are the last man in the world whom I could ever be prevailed upon to marry. I would sooner spend the rest of my life tucked away in Hertfordshire, a scorned spinster, than spend another second in company with the likes of you!"

With those words, she hastily fled down the path. The tumult of her mind was now painfully great. Rumours of a scandal—she had brought this on herself, and she surely would suffer the consequences by herself. Her greatest regret was that she had been a complete failure as regarded her purposes in helping Jane.

Her head pounded. *How might I possibly face Mr. Bingley now? Surely, as Mr. Darcy's closest friend, he must know of my foolish actions. Who else knows? Lord Latham? Lady Gwendolen?*

Tired and weak, she sat and cried for half an hour. *Who is at the heart of this rumour? Is the situation as dire as Mr. Darcy proclaims?*

Her astonishment as she reflected on what had passed was increased by every review of it. That she should receive an offer of marriage from Mr. Darcy! That he should have been in love with her for months! So much in love as to wish to marry her despite the objections that had led to his preventing Mr. Bingley's marrying Jane. Having inspired such strong affection was somewhat gratifying.

She thought it was only fitting that he should feel the sting of rejection as painfully as had her sister. Nevertheless, she could not be wholly satisfied for if she would but admit it, she had sensed the attraction and been on her way to some semblance of reciprocity. However, his brazen declaration of what he had done with respect to Jane, and the unfeeling manner in which he had mentioned Mr. Wickham. No, it was all entirely too reprehensible.

I shall never forgive him!

Chapter 11

Looking forlorn, Elizabeth sat in the carriage making its way from the manor house, as if saying good-bye forever to that which might have meant something to her. Lady Susan did not know what to make of her young charge. She had arrived at Latham Hall with such high hopes. Looking at her now, one would presume she had lost her best friend in the world.

Lady Susan could only think of one thing that might have happened to bring about such a change. *Lady Gwendolen seemed a little too accommodating in seeing that we might be on our way, not at all disappointed in seeing us take our leave. What a shame. The two young ladies were getting along exceedingly well.*

Elizabeth reminded her of her niece, Madeline, though Elizabeth's prospects were better. After all, Elizabeth was a gentleman's daughter—even if he was a lowly country gentleman. Her roots in trade were a knock against her, as well, thus Lady Susan's purpose in trying to match her with Sir Robert Boxley. He was a decent, respectable man, and a landowner of adequate means. To her ladyship's way of thinking, the match was advantageous for all concerned.

Now witnessing Elizabeth's despair, Lady Susan pontificated upon her view of what had occurred. "I pray our precipitous leave-taking has nothing to do with Mr. Darcy, my dear."

To Elizabeth's confused look, she continued. "One would have to be blind not to have discerned how he attended you last evening. My dear, you are aware of the fact that Lady Gwendolen has her heart set on the gentleman. The whole world knows that. Have you and her ladyship quarrelled?

"As much as I adore you—adore you both, I do believe Lady Gwendolen loves him best. She remains unattached not for want of suitable prospects, I assure you."

Elizabeth smiled weakly. "You need not be concerned in that regard. Should Mr. Darcy and Lady Gwendolen decide to live their lives as husband and wife, I shall not be the least bit disheartened." Elizabeth sounded as if she might have been trying to persuade herself instead of Lady Susan.

80808003

He stood in the doorway and observed her as she busied herself arranging a bouquet of fresh-cut flowers. He knocked to get her attention.

"You wanted to see me, Lady Gwendolen?"

"Mr. Darcy!" She smoothed her gown and patted her hair. "Oh, yes, Mr. Darcy. Please come in. Have a seat."

Walking into the room, cutting half the distance between them, he stopped. "Lady Gwendolen, what is this about?"

"Mr. Darcy, I cannot help noticing that you have been keeping to yourself the past two days. Has something occurred to upset you?"

"I am bothered, yes, though you need not concern yourself."

"Will you not tell me what it is? Perhaps I might be of service. You will find me an enthusiastic listener. I am afraid my brother is quite distracted with ... other guests." She wanted but dared not give voice to the true reason for her brother's preoccupation.

"Yes, I know. I am afraid there is nothing you can do for me, Lady Gwendolen."

"Why must you be aloof with me, Mr. Darcy? Surely, my brother has told you how much I esteem you."

"I am not sure this is a conversation you and I need to have." His voice resonated with caution warranted by such an exchange.

"Why not? Must I wait forever for you to take notice of me?

"I do notice you," Darcy said in earnest. "I also know your brother's wishes as regards the two of us. However, I believe you deserve better."

"How can you say that?"

"Lady Gwendolen, I never wish to say anything to hurt you. Suffice it to say there is indeed the perfect man for you, someone who will love and cherish you, as you ought to be. You have yet to meet him."

Darcy stood to leave the room. "I am sorry. Please, excuse me. I must be getting back to my room. In fact, I mean to speak with your brother to let him know I plan to cut my visit short. Bingley and I talked, and since he is here largely at my request, he plans to accompany me back to town."

"Oh, Mr. Darcy, you know I had such high hopes for this week."

"Yes I know, and I do not mean to upset you in any way. I must be going. Good day."

Lady Gwendolen cried out in distress, stopping Darcy in his footsteps. Tears attendant of one forced to witness her dreams unravel misted her eyes. He returned to console her, mindful of decorum and unwilling to do anything that might be misconstrued.

He guided her to sit beside him on the settee. "Tell me, Lady Gwendolen, what is this about? Why the tears?"

"Must I say it? You must know I am in love with you, and that I have been for years."

"No, I know no such thing. I suspect your sentiments are borne out of infatuation, not love. You do not know me well enough to profess such a powerful sentiment as love."

"I know what I feel. I struggle each day not to spend it in thoughts of you. I am sure of my love for you."

"I am sure you are mistaken. Take heart, Lady Gwendolen. I hold you in considerable esteem, but that is the extent of my feelings for you.

"You must accept that. Tell me that you do."

"Mr. Darcy, you can say what you will. I know my own heart."

"I suppose you think you do. I must confess I know my own, as well. One woman, alone, holds my heart."

"Is it Miss Elizabeth? Is Miss Elizabeth Bennet the woman of whom you speak?"

Darcy was silent. Lady Gwendolen looked into his eyes. "Your silence is confirmation."

"I will always hold you in esteem, Lady Gwendolen. However, I will not allow you to cling to hope for that which will never be."

In silence, his eyes pierced deeply into to hers. For a long moment, he wondered if the pain he had unintentionally inflicted upon her was akin to the pain he suffered in having lost his chance with Elizabeth ... pain inherent in a love that would never be.

The hopeful look in her eyes suggested that her ladyship misread his remorse. If she did not listen, if she continued to cling to hope in spite of his declaration, there was nothing more he could say for he did not mean to hurt her.

Darcy stood and spoke softly. "I will leave you now." He reached for her hand and raised it slightly, nothing more. He bowed. He released her hand and quit the room.

Agitated, he halted in his steps halfway down the grand hall. *That voice!*

"Pardon me, Mr. Darcy, might I have a word with you?"

He was on his way to speak to his friend about his plans to leave Latham Hall, but the sound of her calling out to him forced him to turn and look back to see her standing in the doorway of the library.

"Duchess?"

She beckoned him to join her. Once inside, she promptly locked the door. "I do not wish to be interrupted. Do you mind?"

"What is this about?"

"I need your assistance in a rather delicate matter regarding Trevor. I wish for you to have a word with him on my behalf."

"I swore off involvement in your affairs years ago, or did you forget?"

"No, I remember all too well. Still, I need you. I want you to speak with him and persuade him to desist in this notion of his that I shall ever be his wife."

"If you have no intentions of doing anything other than dallying with him, then why not leave him alone. Why did you come this week?"

"Believe me, I was sorely tempted to remain in town, but Trevor assured me that things would be different, and that he would no longer try to pressure me into marrying him."

"Please spare me the sordid details."

"You asked."

Changing tactics, the Duchess approached him and laced her arm through his. She attempted to coax him to have a seat, but he did not budge.

Dropping his arm, she laced her voice with honey instead. "Mr. Darcy, I have no desire to argue with you, and there is no reason we should not be friends. I do not endeavour to cause Trevor pain. I enjoy our time together immensely.

"The fact is that I have no wish, nor any reason, to marry again. It does not mean I do not care deeply for him."

"You are wasting your time with me. Trevor knows my opinion on the matter. If you are unhappy with any pressure he is bringing to bear with the intention of making you his wife, you should address those concerns directly with him."

"Oh! Why did I bother to think you might be of service to me? You always looked down on me, even when I became the Duchess of Sexton. To you, I was unfailingly the unfortunate, poverty-stricken daughter of a drunken, gambling shell of a man who made his entire family ridiculous."

"You saw yourself as such. Do not ascribe your low opinion of yourself to me. Besides, I was prepared to overlook your diminished circumstances in deference to my friend's adoration of you."

"What is changed? He adores me still. However, you abhor my very presence."

"Everything changed when you cast him aside for the Duke of Sexton, a man three times your senior, for motives that were clearly mercenary. Why settle for an earl when you might have a duke?"

"Trevor does not hold my choice against me. He understood that my father forced me into marrying the Duke. My family might have suffered ruination pursuant to my father's gambling and drinking. Even the Helmsley family fortune was not enough to dig my family out of the dire straits my father had settled upon us."

"Then what is stopping you now? Now, when you have wealth and status, you continue to string my friend along when, in your heart, you know you will never marry him."

"This arrangement of ours affords him all the benefits of marriage, and it affords me all the freedom and security of determining my own fate. Why would I give that up?"

"You are unbelievably selfish."

"You are one to talk, Mr. Darcy. I am sure it vexes you exceedingly to be always forced to be in my company whenever you visit Trevor."

"You give yourself too much credit, Duchess. Your presence has no effect upon me one way or the other. Good day, *Your Grace*."

ಬಚಬಚಬಚ

"Darcy, I know we have had scarcely a moment alone since Miss Elizabeth took her leave, what with Juliette's arrival."

Darcy sipped his drink in silence.

"When you left my study that morning, I was sure you had made up your mind to protect Miss Elizabeth from scandal by proposing to her. Was I correct in supposing such a thing?"

"I am not engaged, if that is what you are asking."

"You speak as if that is a bad thing. Clearly, you admire her. Even Gwendolen could discern that. However, did you seriously consider what it would mean had she accepted your proposal?"

"I confess it is a bad thing. I more than admire Miss Elizabeth. I love her. Not only have I failed her when what I meant to do was protect her, I have offended her."

"I am sorry to hear of your suffering, my friend. Is there something I might do as regards Miss Elizabeth? Speak with her, perhaps?"

Darcy finished his drink and set his glass aside. "Trevor, I did not come here seeking advice in that regard, as much as I respect you and value our friendship. I will find a way to make things up to Miss Elizabeth. I need your help in unmasking the source of this troublesome information. Once we learn the source, proper steps can be taken to stop it from spreading any further."

"Fear not. I have some idea of the origins of this information. I will handle it."

"I am in your debt." Darcy stood to take his leave. "I suspect your sister will require a bit more of your attention this afternoon than you have given her of late. I have come from speaking with her."

"Is Gwendolen terribly upset?"

"I attempted to explain things to her; however, I suspect she clings to some semblance of hope, still."

"I shall speak with my sister."

"I have one other thing. You know I am loath to interfere when it comes to your situation with the Duchess—"

"She is not your favourite person; yes, I am aware of that fact."

"Nevertheless, I urge you to speak with her, as well. What is more, I suggest you listen."

Lord Latham remained silent, pensive. Darcy walked towards the door and then stopped to face his friend.

"Bingley and I take our leave in half an hour. Shall I see you in town, in a day or so?"

"Yes, absolutely, my old friend. Pray I have good news to report."

৩১৩১৩১

Darcy reread the meticulous results of several hours spent on his letter-writing campaign since returning to London, days ahead of his originally planned arrival. His sentiments varied widely from anger to rage, from disappointment to resolve. He began by assuring Elizabeth in the coldest of tones that he did not intend to repeat any of his previous declarations. His character alone, of which she thought so little, demanded he address in full the accusations she made against him—nothing more.

Therein, he wrote of his role in separating his friend from Miss Bennet; however, he had not learned to think his actions were unwarranted, and even though Elizabeth's words on her sister's sentiments must certainly bear some consideration, they were not enough to convince him of her impartiality.

He spoke at length of her accusations that he had been the cause of George Wickham's diminished circumstances. Even as Darcy read the letter to himself, he knew it would never find its way into Elizabeth's hands.

What would be the point? In spite of her words arguing her sister's love for Bingley, were it in my power to do it all again, I would behave no differently.

Bingley deserves better, if he is to earn a place befitting his wealth and long sought after standing amongst Society. How might I in good conscience encourage such an alliance merely borne out of an affection of only a few weeks? The situation of Mrs. Bennet's family being in trade, though objectionable, is nothing in comparison to the total want of propriety displayed by the entire family, save Elizabeth and Miss Bennet.

Besides that, he had often seen his friend in love before. He concluded this time was no different.

Darcy pondered the irony. To Bingley, he had been better than he had been to himself. Though he would not encourage Bingley in aligning with such a family, he knew he would jump at such a prospect for himself.

The strongest reason he could not bring himself to deliver the letter, though, had nothing to do with impropriety and everything to do with his young sister. Darcy surmised Elizabeth viewed his sister with circumspection already, thinking she was the reason he did not covet an alliance between Bingley and Miss Jane Bennet. He did not know how she would react in hearing such an account from him, someone she thought so little of, against her favourite, George Wickham, whom she obviously held in esteem.

Besides, the story was not his to tell.

Darcy balled the letter in his hands and tossed it into the fire. As much as he wished to give Elizabeth a true account of George Wickham's character, he would not betray his sister's confidence.

He stood before the fire and looked on as the words on the pages melted into nonexistence, as if never committed to paper, forever safe from perusal. There had to be another way.

As stubborn as Elizabeth is, the fact remains, something has to be done about our situation.

Darcy walked to his desk, sat in his chair, and rested his head in his hands in deep contemplation.

He looked up when Georgiana entered his study. Her face bore a worried expression. He credited himself as the cause of her concern having marked its onset with his return from the Latham country estate.

"Brother, it has been too long since we entertained anyone at Darcy House, do you not agree?"

"Indeed, though the thought of entertaining Miss Bingley and the Hursts holds little appeal for me. We can hardly escape them should we invite Bingley to dinner."

"Actually, I was not thinking of Mr. Bingley at all, though I would welcome his company."

"Whom do you have in mind?"

"I am of a mind to invite Miss Elizabeth Bennet, and her Uncle and Aunt Gardiner, of course. I have meant to for a while. Now seems the perfect time. I would like to extend the invitation before we leave for Kent."

"No," Darcy said without thought. "I mean to say an invitation to dinner will not be feasible."

"Why is it unfeasible? Do you not wish to see Miss Elizabeth again? Though you will not admit it, I know the disappointment you suffered when she left our home without seeing you that morning."

"Actually, Georgiana, I have seen Miss Elizabeth. In fact, she and I were together at Lord Latham's party. I am afraid we parted on less than favourable terms."

Darcy walked back to the fireplace and stared into the flames. All evidence of his disappointed hopes had vanished. "The truth is I believe I am the last person in the world whom Miss Elizabeth would wish to see. I have no one to blame but myself … and one George Wickham." His last words were beneath his breath.

George Wickham. Months had passed since he had last uttered those two words in his sister's presence. The last thing he wanted was to revisit what had been one of the most painful moments of their lives, save the loss of their father. If she heard him, she pretended otherwise.

"I am sorry to hear that the two of you are at odds, Brother. I like Miss Elizabeth. I had hoped to become better acquainted with her."

Darcy smiled. Despite the fact that he had offered Elizabeth his hand in marriage out of obligation, he had also done it out of love. He loved her. He wanted to spend the rest of his life with her.

"I know."

Georgiana placed a light kiss on her brother's cheek. "Do you mind if I take the carriage? I need to see someone."

"I trust you will be accompanied by Mrs. Annesley, young lady."

"Yes, of course, Brother. I would never venture to leave the house without her."

⬥⬥⬥

Elizabeth suffered a surprise when the housekeeper announced her visitor.

"Miss Darcy, welcome. I apologise for my aunt's being out. Did you come all this way unescorted?"

"You need not apologise, Miss Elizabeth. I came here to see you. Thank you for receiving me. I confess to not travelling across town alone. However, I asked my companion, Mrs. Annesley, to take advantage of my visit with you to call on her relatives who live nearby. What I have to discuss is of delicate nature."

"Please be seated." Elizabeth gestured toward the sofa. "I was about to have tea. Will you join me?"

"Yes, thank you."

Elizabeth prepared the tea and handed her guest a cup. Elizabeth had not seen the young lady since she visited her with Mr. Darcy's physician in tow at the start of the Season.

"Pray what brings you so far this morning?" Elizabeth said. She suspected it might have to do with Mr. Darcy. What other purposes might there be?

"I will be honest with you. I am here because of something my brother said to me this morning."

"Your brother?" Elizabeth did not expect the young lady to be that upfront. "Did your brother tell you what transpired between us earlier this week?" Elizabeth fiddled with her napkin, uneasy by the prospect.

"No. He only went as far as to say the two of you had seen each other at Lord Latham's party, and you had not parted on good terms."

Elizabeth said nothing. She sipped her tea in relief. The last thing she needed was a lecture from Mr. Darcy's sister, advocating for or against his *chivalrous* proposal. She did not know the young lady well enough to know which way she leaned.

Georgiana put Elizabeth's busy mind at ease. "He also spoke of your knowing Mr. Wickham."

"Indeed. I made Mr. Wickham's acquaintance in Meryton, shortly after meeting your brother."

"Miss Elizabeth, my brother hinted at your opinion of him being coloured by your acquaintance with Mr. Wickham."

"Miss Darcy, at the expense of sounding rude, I am not inclined to discuss my opinion of either of the two gentlemen with you."

"I understand your sentiments; believe me, I do. However, I cannot allow you to maintain an opinion of my brother based on Mr. Wickham's account. I assure you, my brother is the best of men."

Elizabeth smiled and took another sip of tea, signalling Georgiana to continue her speech.

"Though I know nothing of the particulars of how Mr. Wickham went about poisoning your mind against my brother, I know enough of how much he dislikes my brother to warrant suspicion. You see, he employed similar tactics with me."

"Miss Darcy—"

She held up her hand. "Please hear what I am about to say. My father loved Mr. Wickham. He educated him, and he even bequeathed him the living in Kympton in his will."

Elizabeth suspected where the conversation was headed. "I have knowledge of this, for Mr. Wickham told me as much himself."

"I do not doubt that. I am sure he told you my brother

denied him the living."

"Did he not, Miss Darcy?"

"I will not attempt to deny it. However, my brother did not act as he did without good reason, causes of which I was wholly unaware at the time. Mr. Wickham also had told me that my brother had done him a great disservice. He preyed upon the tender regard that I had held for him since I was a child. He preyed upon my wish to make amends for what my brother had done.

"I later learned Mr. Wickham never had any attention of accepting the living and having told my brother as much, accepted three thousand pounds in lieu of it only to squander the entirety of the funds. He returned to Pemberley demanding more, but my brother refused to give him any more money.

"I might never have known any of this except Mr. Wickham followed me to Ramsgate, pledging violent love for me. I agreed to an elopement. Before we could put the scheme in effect, my brother arrived in Ramsgate.

"Though I believed I was in love with Mr. Wickham, I could not in good conscience deceive my brother. I told him of our plans.

"Never had I witnessed such dismay, such disappointment in my brother's eyes. However, that was nothing compared to the ensuing rage in him when Mr. Wickham arrived to spirit me away to Gretna Green.

"My brother confronted Mr. Wickham and accused him of taking advantage of an innocent for his own malicious purposes. The two argued. In scarcely the work of a few moments, Mr. Wickham admitted his duplicity. His being in Ramsgate had nothing to do with his love for me and everything to do with his hatred of my brother. The way he went on to account for his motives is too hurtful for me to describe. Suffice it to say, he admitted that if not for my fortune of thirty thousand pounds, he would not have given me a second thought.

"My shame was great. Had it not been for my brother's love and his constant reassurances that I was not to blame for succumbing to the seduction of an older, worldlier man, I know not what would have become of me. Some months have passed since I learned to think similarly."

Elizabeth thought of everything she knew of Wickham. One by one, all her past arguments in his favour melted away by the obvious pain in Georgiana's face in having to recount his misdeeds. She thought of Miss King; how she had turned a sympathetic eye to his desire to marry her to raise his own standing in life. She, too, suffered the sting of shame made worse by the guilt of duplicity. What she had perceived as allowable with one woman was clearly mercenary, nay cruelty, when directed towards the young and innocent Miss Darcy.

"Miss Darcy," she said, "I am sorry. I never knew, never suspected anyone capable of such depravity."

"No, how could you? I did not tell you this to garner your sympathy, Miss Elizabeth. I only told you that you might have a better indication of my brother's character ... that you would not judge him harshly on the word of Mr. Wickham."

Elizabeth thought about the many times she had prided herself on her discernment, yet she had praised Mr. Wickham whilst abusing Mr. Darcy, not only to others but also to his face. Embarrassed and ashamed, she wondered if she even knew herself. What was worse, she had not been as gracious to Miss Darcy as she ought, but rather had returned the young woman's attempts to show her kindness with cool civility.

Soon, the Gardiner's maid bearing a letter for Elizabeth interrupted the two ladies.

Elizabeth took it in hand and perused it. "This letter is from Mary, my sister."

"Then, I shall prepare to take my leave. You must be eager to read what she has to say. I need only send word to my driver."

"No—no, please do not leave right away, Miss Darcy, unless you are expected elsewhere." Elizabeth thought if nothing else she might find a means of conveying her regrets to Mr. Darcy by paying off every arrear of kindness to his sister.

"I have nowhere else to be."

"Very well; if you will pardon me, I will see to it our tea is freshened." Elizabeth placed the letter from Mary in her pocket and carried the tea service to the kitchen. Whilst waiting for the Gardiner's maid to prepare a fresh pot of boiling water, she sat at the table to peruse Mary's letter. Though she did not wish to let on to her guest, it bothered her that Mary had sent the letter by express.

Not long thereafter, Elizabeth reminded herself to breathe as she stood on the opposite side of the door. *My family is ruined!* She put on a brave face and pushed forward. Walking into the room, she decided it best to conceal the truth from Miss Darcy. Alas, the young woman proved as astute an observer as her brother had ever been.

Georgiana went to Elizabeth's side and placed her hand on Elizabeth's arm. "Miss Elizabeth, what is it? You look as if you have seen a ghost!"

Elizabeth burst into tears. Georgiana put her arm around Elizabeth's shoulder and led her to take a seat. After a minute or so, the maid entered the room bearing the tray.

"Thank you, I shall handle things," Georgiana said to the young maid in response to her confusion, whilst Elizabeth turned away, attempting to compose herself. Upon the maid's quitting the room, Georgiana prepared a cup of tea and handed it to Elizabeth.

"Please, drink this."

Elizabeth attempted a measured smile. After a moment, she said, "Thank you, Miss Darcy."

"You are troubled. Please, tell me what has occurred? Has

something happened at home with your family? Is that what has wrought such a change in your demeanour?"

"Oh, Miss Darcy, the news from home is grave ... grave indeed. I do not think it would be fair to burden you."

"You need not worry on my behalf. Is there anything I might do?"

"I fear there is nothing to be done. You see, my youngest sister has run away. She has thrown herself in the power—" Elizabeth looked into Georgiana's eyes. "My sister, Lydia, has thrown herself into Mr. Wickham's power."

Georgiana's haunted countenance struck Elizabeth with force. The two young ladies embraced, neither sure of which one comforted the other.

ꙅꙅꙅ

Georgiana ran into her brother's study, no longer able to countenance the brave face she had donned as she had left the Gardiner's home. It seemed too real. The pain. The humiliation she had suffered in Ramsgate. Everything coming back at once. Haunting her once again. Darcy stood upon her entrance, welcomed her into his embrace as she ran across the room.

"Georgiana," he said, "please tell me at once. What has happened to upset you so?"

Trembling, Georgiana suffered as truly as if her worst nightmare had revisited her doorstep. The warmth of her brother's arms reminded her she was safe. He had saved her. Perhaps he might accomplish the impossible once again. Pulling herself together, wiping her tears with the back of her hand, she accepted his proffered handkerchief.

"Brother, I know you told me that I should not visit Miss Elizabeth, but I was unable to refrain."

Panic etched across his face. Deny it if he wished, but his sister could see how much he cared for Miss Elizabeth.

"No harm has befallen Miss Elizabeth."

"Then what is the matter? Something has upset you."

"I am afraid the news from Cheapside is dreadful. Miss Elizabeth swore me to secrecy, yet I am certain I must make an exception."

"What is it?"

"Her youngest sister, Miss Lydia, has ... has left the protection of her family and run off with Mr. Wickham. Miss Elizabeth is devastated by this scandalous turn of events, and what it must mean for her family. She fears all hope is lost."

Chapter 12

The Longbourn household settled into a quiet uproar. Elizabeth's mother, despite having retired to her bed upon learning of her Lydia's actions, could find no peace. Her mother's misery, however, had been nothing compared to the despair of those around her. Mrs. Bennet had made certain of it. Elizabeth relaxed at last. Her mother slept.

Her father had gone to town within a day of discovering Lydia's letter announcing her intended elopement with Mr. Wickham to Gretna Green, to do what he told Elizabeth he never thought he would ever have to do when he opened his home to the nefarious lieutenant. Her father's foray into town had only compounded her mother's worry, for Mrs. Bennet was certain he would be forced to fight the villainous Mr. Wickham; he most certainly would be killed. What would become of them?

Upon his quick return from town, several days later, to Elizabeth, Mr. Bennet's face reflected resignation. He seemed to have aged several years in the few days since venturing to town. Elizabeth studied her father's countenance, his posture, his demeanour. What a toll this endeavour had taken on him, her father, a man who would have been content to pass the bulk of his remaining days on earth in the comfort of his library. Moreover, by his telling, it had all been in vain, for he and Mr. Gardiner had met one dead-end after another in their quest for information. All evidence suggested one thing; the couple had not travelled to Gretna Green. All leads proved false, as though they had vanished to the underside of nowhere at all.

Since her own hasty return from town on the same afternoon that she received the letter from home telling of Lydia's elopement, Elizabeth and Mary had formed a kindred regard in the care of their mother. Jane kept to herself. Kitty did too, having stated her belief as she did that had she spoken up, she might have prevented her sister's foolishness. Elizabeth noted her younger sister's sentiments as a stark contrast to her mother in that regard. Mrs. Bennet blamed everyone else for the fiasco, and often lamented on how things had come to this when all she ever wanted was to see her five daughters well settled.

Her complaints against Elizabeth were just as strident as they had been before Elizabeth ventured to town to visit the Gardiners. What sorrow she had endured over the past several months! She recited her pride in the notion of her first-born daughter being the mistress of the neighbouring estate of Netherfield Park and the security she had enjoyed when she believed her second eldest daughter would be married to the heir of their family's estate. The first union was destined to put her remaining daughters in the paths of other rich men; the second, to secure her place in her beloved home for the remainder of her days. Two perfect unions—her life's work nearly done.

Despite the deathblow wielded upon her hopes for her two eldest daughters, as far as Elizabeth could detect, her mother had managed to recover owing to the fact that there was still time. Elizabeth feared this latest setback was too much for her mother to bear, for even a nonsensical woman could not deny the damage to the rest of them wrought by her youngest daughter's thoughtless act.

Two days after their father's return from town, Elizabeth and Mary sat on either side of their mother's bed and watched her sleep.

"Lizzy, I hesitate to ask, in light of everything that has occurred with Lydia. Yet, my curiosity begs satisfaction. Did you meet Mr. Bingley whilst in town?"

The memories of her argument with Mr. Darcy flooded Elizabeth's mind. "Mary, perhaps we might take a stroll about the garden whilst Mama rests."

"Sunshine and a breath of fresh air would serve us both well," Mary said.

Once outside in the embrace of the sun, Elizabeth was at leisure to talk. "Mary, I met Mr. Bingley whilst visiting Lady Gwendolen Helmsley at her brother's country estate."

"Were you able to speak with him? Does he care for Jane?"

"In all honesty, I cannot say. I mean to say he and I had no chance to speak privately." Elizabeth looked away, wistfully. "Mr. Darcy was there."

"Oh! Is that why you were unable to speak with Mr. Bingley in confidence?"

"Well, in a manner of speaking. I learned Mr. Darcy had a greater role to play in separating Mr. Bingley and Jane than I ever had suspected. I discovered the truth of the extent of his role whilst in Tilbury. I confronted him; we argued. I am afraid he and I parted on the worst of terms."

"Lizzy, I fail to understand how an argument with Mr. Darcy thwarted your efforts to speak with Mr. Bingley. The two of you were always at odds. I would have supposed an altercation with Mr. Darcy would only bolster your determination."

"Actually, the argument with Mr. Darcy was predicated upon a number of matters, things I hesitate to discuss, except to say I wanted nothing more than to flee his presence and return to London as soon as could be."

"I suppose everything turned out for the best. I should not expect Mr. Bingley to return to Jane's side now, not with the shame Lydia has brought on the family."

Elizabeth and Mary rounded the corner and espied their father heading into the house with a letter in hand, having received it moments earlier by express. They raced towards him.

"Papa, Papa," they breathlessly spoke in unison upon reaching his side.

"Papa, is that a letter from town?" Elizabeth said. "Has my uncle had any success? Have Lydia and Mr. Wickham been discovered?"

"Will they be married?" Mary said.

"Everything has been arranged," Elizabeth's father said. "The financial burden of this scandal upon your uncle's purse has been substantial; nonetheless, everything has been arranged."

They had not dared wish for such happy news. Lydia married, even to a scoundrel, was better than the alternative.

"Come; let us share the news with Mama!"

"Shall we wait until she awakens?"

"I suppose we should let her be, for now. She has barely rested since this scandal broke. Nevertheless, we must tell someone. The news is too good to keep to ourselves, do you not agree?"

"Let us tell Jane. This must certainly lift her spirits a bit."

"Yes, and Kitty will want to hear the news, as well. She has been quite distraught."

Elizabeth and Mary nearly collided with Jane, as they headed up the stairs. "Jane!"

"I heard a commotion. Has something happened?" Jane placed her hand on Elizabeth's. "Dearest Lizzy, I want to do what I might in support of our family during this crisis. You and Mary have taken too much upon yourselves. I have come to realise my troubles are nothing by comparison to poor Lydia's, and I can no longer escape, in good conscience, those responsibilities that come with being the eldest daughter. How might I help?"

Elizabeth embraced her sister. "Oh, Jane! I am delighted to witness this improvement in your spirits, and what Mary and I have to say will surely raise them even further. You see, we have spoken with Papa. He says Lydia is to be married!"

"Married? Do not mistake me, for I am relieved, but how? When did this come about?"

"Papa says our uncle has handled everything—at a considerable expense to himself, I might add."

"How much do you suppose this business cost?"

"I dare say Wickham would be a fool to settle for less than ten thousand pounds." Even as Elizabeth voiced the words, she still deemed the scheme unfathomable. Jane and Mary forced their mouths shut.

"Mama will want to know about the wedding."

"Mary and I agree. We thought we might allow her to rest. We shall tell her as soon as she wakes."

"Mama is awake. I left her side a minute ago."

Oh, the healing power of words proclaiming the marriage of one of her daughters! Mrs. Bennet jumped out of her bed and blethered about. So much needed to be done. A wedding!

"My Lydia will be married, and to such a fine young man." Mrs. Bennet raced to her wardrobe in search of what to wear. "I do hope they settle in a nearby estate."

Elizabeth hid her true sentiments behind a half-hearted smile. If her mother only realised the sort of man her youngest daughter was marrying, would she be nearly as pleased? Elizabeth shook her head in frustration. No doubt, her mother would be equally appeased.

Not too many days thereafter, her mother's delight in receiving her youngest daughter and her new son-in-law at Longbourn was overshadowed by her sadness that they would be going the next day to Newcastle. Her father's sentiments were quite the opposite. Mr. Wickham had deceived him. Repeatedly, he said he was not apt to forget, or forgive, the young man's betrayal any time soon.

Elizabeth showed her disdain for her new brother-in-law by scarcely uttering a word to him that he did not labour to earn. When conversation with the gentleman was unavoidable, some mention of the Darcys was made, given Wickham's knowledge of Elizabeth having spent time in town. When Elizabeth confirmed his supposition that she must have run across Mr. Darcy at some point, he prodded her into going a step further.

"I also had the pleasure of spending quite a bit of time in Miss Darcy's company."

"I wonder, Lizzy, how did you find Miss Darcy?" How it vexed her that he had the right to address her so, as they were now brother and sister.

"To be honest, I have to say she was nothing as you described her."

"I do not doubt it. I imagine she has grown kindlier with age."

"Kindlier, indeed, and far wiser, I dare say."

His stricken countenance allowed Elizabeth to discern she had hit her mark, and she walked away with the satisfaction of having let him know that she knew what he was about.

Escaping conversation with Lydia was impossible. The

family sat around the drawing room on the last evening that the newly married couple would be guests at Longbourn, listening to Lydia go on and on about the happy state of being a married woman, even going as far as to recommend the institution of marriage to her sisters.

Brooding fleetingly, she opined there had been a moment when she supposed the marriage would not happen. "Thank goodness for Mr. Darcy's being there—"

Elizabeth, who had scarcely paid attention to a word her sister had spoken that evening suddenly took note. She looked up in time to witness Mr. Wickham nudge his wife to be quiet. Puzzled, Elizabeth wondered why Mr. Darcy was at Lydia's wedding.

Wickham quickly changed the subject, speaking instead of his enthusiasm for his new commission. Too late. Elizabeth was sure she had heard her sister say Mr. Darcy was at the wedding, and she was determined to find out what she meant.

Elizabeth later came upon her youngest sister in the hallway. She quickly approached her. "Lydia, did I understand you to say Mr. Darcy was at your wedding? Why would Mr. Darcy be at your wedding?"

Lydia laughed. Placing her hand to her lips, she said, "Why would I say such a thing, Lizzy? You know my Wickham does not like Mr. Darcy. Everyone knows that." She smirked and lowered her voice. "Besides, it is supposed to be a great secret."

Wickham hurriedly joined Elizabeth and Lydia upon espying them speaking in hushed whispers and grabbed his wife by her elbow.

"Say good night to your sister." His tone was brutish and intimidating, and he led her away with a little too much enthusiasm, leaving Elizabeth standing there, aghast, her mouth wide opened.

She shook her head. *Poor Lydia.*

Chapter 13

With the excitement of the past weeks, it had slipped everyone's attention that Kitty was to accompany Miss Maria Lucas to Hunsford to visit her sister, Charlotte, and her sister's husband, Mr. Collins.

Lydia's actions had the unintended consequence of a sterner, more conscientious Mr. Bennet, who proclaimed that under no circumstances was his next youngest daughter to escape his sight before attaining the age of eighteen.

His edict made for two particularly unhappy young ladies, both of whom had looked forward to the trip with such heightened anticipation. Charlotte had proposed the perfect remedy. If Kitty could not travel to Hunsford, perhaps her dear friend, Eliza, would come in her sister's stead.

Kitty was gravely disappointed with the scheme, but there was nothing to be done about it now, not as long as Mr. Bennet determined to make up for a lifetime of fatherly neglect. Miss Lucas was agreeable. There remained only one person to be persuaded—Elizabeth.

To Charlotte's letter in recommendation of the scheme,

Elizabeth responded:

... So much has changed since your invitation to my sister, Kitty, to accompany your sister to Hunsford. I am reminded of Mr. Collins's letter to my father where he spoke fairly eloquently on the grave affliction all my family was suffering under, and how the demise of my youngest sister would have been a blessing in light of her shame.

Mr. Collins went on to expound how poor Lydia's false step has injured the fortunes of the rest of us, for who will connect themselves with such a family and further congratulated himself on having escaped involvement in such sorrow and disgrace.

Pray tell, dear Charlotte, am I to impart such dishonour upon his doorstep?

Charlotte's response was prompt and succinct, and included words to the following effect:

... My dear husband is cognizant of the wrong that has been righted by Lydia's fortuitous marriage, with my having reminded him of the magnificence of Christian forgiveness.

Mind you, my dear Eliza, there is also the matter of my having spoken highly in your favour many times in the presence of Lady Catherine de Bourgh. She looks forward to making your acquaintance, and my husband is ever mindful of attending his noble patroness's every desire.

Dare I beg for the opportunity to entertain my dearest friend in my new home?

Elizabeth responded promptly.

... I shall be happy to visit you in my sister's stead.

Soon enough, a travel date was set.

ಬೊಬೊಬೊ

News of Mr. Bingley's imminent return to Netherfield Park did not take long to reach Mrs. Bennet's hearing, and sooner than she had expected, but much longer than she had wished, he came to call.

One moment, Elizabeth sat next to the window observing Kitty lulling about in the yard, undoubtedly bemoaning her fate. The next moment she looked up as Kitty raced into the room. "Jane, Mama, Mr. Bingley is coming."

Everybody in the room except Jane raced to the window to have a look. Sure enough, it was Mr. Bingley. They would have recognised his blazing red hair from a mile off.

"What a great honour it will be to receive Mr. Bingley! And look, he is not alone." Mrs. Bennet strained her eyes to make out his companion. "Why, it is the proud, disagreeable Mr. Darcy. What on earth is *he* thinking in coming here?"

She turned away from the window, rushed to the mirror above the mantel, and smoothed her hair. "What is there to be done now, but to make the best of it? Mr. Bingley is the one who counts."

Turning her attention to Elizabeth and her sisters, she said, "Make haste, everyone. Do not stand there. Take your places. We must not appear too eager."

As soon as the gentlemen were announced, Elizabeth noticed two things as regarded her mother's behaviour towards the guests. She seemed unforgiving towards Mr. Darcy for his rudeness when they had made his acquaintance last year, and towards Mr. Bingley, her every grievance had fallen along the wayside.

Both Jane and Elizabeth were uncomfortable enough merely being in the company of the two gentlemen once again. Elizabeth had said nothing to her sister of even having seen Mr. Darcy during her stay in town, much less, that she had rejected his hand in marriage.

How might she tell Jane of any of that without confiding in her sister her failed purpose in going to town in the first place? Perhaps, had she accomplished her objective in going, she might have been more open with her sister. Now, she would not have to say anything. It seemed Mr. Darcy had heeded her request and purposely brought his friend to call on her sister as a means of atonement for his officiousness in separating them.

Elizabeth did not know what to think and decided, instead, to be a quiet studier of the unfolding events.

Once again, Elizabeth suffered the shame of having a mother who wore her opinion of the two gentlemen proudly upon her sleeves. Mrs. Bennet had resolved to be civil to Mr. Darcy, allowing as he was Mr. Bingley's friend. She was failing miserably.

When able to act with impunity, Elizabeth rested her eyes upon the object of her regret. He looked serious and nowhere near as comfortable as she remembered seeing him their last evening together at Lord Latham's estate, when he had been charming and attentive. How could she blame him? Every word her mother ventured to speak in assurance of Mr. Bingley's comfort, she appended with a snide remark intended for Mr. Darcy.

Elizabeth watched in horror as her mother ingratiated herself with Mr. Bingley by talking of the local happenings since he returned to town, including Charlotte's marriage to Mr. Collins and Lydia's marriage to Mr. Wickham.

Her mother's antics, the mention of Mr. Wickham's name, it all recalled Elizabeth to her shame in misjudging Mr. Darcy's character. Elizabeth dared not lift her eyes. Therefore, how Mr. Darcy reacted, she knew not.

Mrs. Bennet went on to complain of the hardship in having her youngest daughter settled far from her home, and her son-in-law's diminished circumstances pursuant to the denial of the rights he ought to have had.

Elizabeth determined to change the subject at once. "Mr. Bingley, do you intend to remain at Netherfield long?"

All eyes were drawn to Elizabeth, including Mr. Darcy's. How she wanted to offer a silent apology, but she knew not how without raising eyebrows. Whilst gazing at Jane wistfully, Bingley responded that he had come down for shooting and planned to remain but a few weeks.

Again, her mother took it upon herself to say something ridiculous in that all the best coveys might be saved for him, if he would but consider shooting on the Longbourn estate, increasing Elizabeth's misery by tenfold at such obsequiousness. She wondered how Jane fared. She suspected her eldest sister suffered an equal measure of embarrassment without knowing for sure. Her sister had only begun to regain a semblance of her former spirits. Though the two had not spoken of Jane's heartbreak since Elizabeth's return, Jane's every action signalled she had resigned herself to her fate, and she did not intend to live the rest of her life being sorry about it.

An end to Elizabeth's mortification was nowhere in sight. Mrs. Bennet continued her copious consideration towards the one gentleman, her cold civility towards the other.

"Mr. Bingley, might I remind you that you are quite in my debt. You promised to take a family dinner with us. I do hope you will join us this evening."

"I shall be delighted to join your family for dinner."

The broad smile that brightened Mrs. Bennet's face disappeared when she turned to his friend. "You are welcome to join us, too, Mr. Darcy." Her manner of speaking, however, belied the sincerity of her invitation.

"I am honoured by your offer. However, I cannot accept it. I am to return to town later today."

Elizabeth's pulse quickened at the sight of Mr. Darcy arising from his seat.

Bingley looked conflicted. "Shall I accompany you back to Netherfield and see you off?"

"I rather suppose you would much prefer to stay and

enjoy your present company. I shall be off to London in but a few hours."

After he had disappeared through the doorway, Elizabeth kicked herself. He had come all this way. Surely, it must count for something.

Do not sit here, her regretful heart shouted. *Make some excuse, whatever excuse is necessary. Do not leave it like this.*

"Please pardon me, Mama, Mr. Bingley, Jane ... I need a breath of fresh air."

By the time Elizabeth walked out the door, any sign of Mr. Darcy's having been there had vanished. Deciding to walk anyway, she set about on an overgrown path towards the grove. There she found comfort in the shade of a large oak tree. She sat and folded her arms over her knees. Thoughts of everything that took place all but placated her mind.

What was his purpose in coming? Surely, he did not come only to be silent, grave, and indifferent. Was it merely to accompany his friend? Did his visit have nothing to do with the hope of seeing me? Have I lost his good opinion forever?

After a while, she stood to return to the house. Mr. Darcy appeared directly ahead of her in the path. Both smiled awkwardly, as befitted the first occasion of their being alone since their bitter argument. They walked towards each other in silent acquiescence.

"Mr. Darcy, I thought you had left for Netherfield Park."

"No. Actually, I have been enjoying the view from the pond. I must beg your pardon. I wanted a moment alone. Mrs. Bennet—your mother, I suppose I am not one of her favourite people."

Elizabeth felt the colour rise in her cheeks. She understood his sentiments too well. Her mother had been everything accommodating and pleasant to Mr. Bingley, and unaccommodating to the point of being rude to Mr. Darcy.

"Forgive me, Miss Elizabeth. I had not intended to be unfeeling."

"You have no need to apologise to me. I believe I should be thanking you for bringing Mr. Bingley here to see my sister."

The two begin a slow pace back towards Longbourn House.

"You need not thank me. Bingley spoke of his desire to return to Hertfordshire after having seen you at Lord Latham's home. He sought my opinion on the matter, and I said I would be happy to accompany him."

"Is that everything you said, Mr. Darcy?"

"I am afraid so, Miss Elizabeth."

"The material point is he has returned."

"Yes, that is the point. Let us hope for a happy resolution for both your sister and my friend."

"As happy as I am for Mr. Bingley's return, will he not be a bit disappointed in your leaving so soon upon your arrival?"

Elizabeth felt an accustomed uncertainty by the look he bestowed. Could he tell that her question of disappointment had more to do with her own sentiments?

"I imagine it seems I am rushing off. However, I have prior plans I can postpone no longer. I have every intention of returning. All things considered, it is probably for the best that I leave. Bingley does not need the distraction of entertaining me, when he had better spend his time—"

Elizabeth interrupted, "I shall not be here to watch over the happy couple either. I, too, have made plans to be elsewhere."

"May I enquire of your plans?"

"Do you remember my friend Charlotte?"

"Yes, I do remember her. Your mother spoke of her having married."

"She is now married to my cousin, Mr. Collins. I am to visit them in Hunsford."

Mr. Darcy smiled. "Then, I have good cause to hope we shall soon be in each other's company again. Georgiana and I will be guests at Rosings Park."

Elizabeth smiled faintly as she dared to hope they might have a second chance.

"Pray tell me my news does not disappoint you, Miss Elizabeth, to know we shall be in proximity soon."

"No. I welcome a chance of spending time with Miss Darcy again."

"She will be delighted to know that. She is fond of you."

"Indeed. I am rather fond of her, though I did not always express it as well as I should have. I shall endeavour to make amends when next we meet."

"Indeed, I have a bit of fence mending to attend, as well."

The two walked on in quiet companionship until they came to the gate, for Elizabeth's part, planning what their next meeting would bring even if she felt a bit unsteady in what seemed an unspoken armistice. Mr. Darcy parted from her in the usual way, and walked in the opposite direction, leaving Elizabeth with a silent prayer that he, too, suffered a heaviness of heart befitting repentant lovers who longed for a brighter tomorrow.

Days later, Elizabeth scurried between her wardrobe and her bed, packing the last of the belongings she wished to take on her trip to Hunsford. She was to be away for three weeks. Jane lent her sister a hand as they also discussed the unfolding courtship with Mr. Bingley.

"Far be it from me to give anyone advice of the heart. However, you are my dearest sister. I wish for nothing more than your happiness. I encourage you to give Mr. Bingley a second chance."

Though keeping her thoughts on the matter to herself, she had observed how Jane had spent her time with Mr. Bingley since his return—guarded, with a measure of hope. Elizabeth sat beside Jane on the bed and took her by the hand.

"Jane, I do not blame you one bit for feeling as you do.

However, anyone who has seen the way he looks at you can see he is in grave danger of falling as much in love with you as ever he was before."

"Mr. Bingley assures me that he shall remain here for as long as it takes, which must be some evidence of his constancy. Though I will allow that I had resolved should he and I ever meet again, it would be as nothing more than casual acquaintances, the fact of his coming back and his willingness to remain here as long as it takes to erase my lingering doubts, fills my heart with joy."

"Oh, Jane, my heart is filled with joy for you. I am certain that, by the time of my return from Hunsford, Mama will be in the midst of planning the grandest wedding the neighbourhood has ever witnessed."

Chapter 14

Elizabeth and Maria had not quite spent a quarter of an hour alone with Charlotte in her parlour when Mr. Collins, a tall, heavy-looking young man of five and twenty, threw opened the door and rushed inside. Out of breath, he bore exciting news that they were invited to tea at Rosings Park that afternoon.

Elizabeth had no doubts on how this must please Maria immensely, for the young lady had anticipated meeting the venerable Lady Catherine de Bourgh with the eagerness of a young maiden being presented at court. Elizabeth's own sentiments were a mixture of anticipation and nervousness. In spite of her recent accord with Mr. Darcy, she did not know what she might expect of him in the company of his august family. Which man would she next meet?

Their party had entered the grand antechamber of Rosings Park when Charlotte remembered what she had neglected to tell her dear friend. With an apologetic smile, Charlotte placed her hand on Elizabeth's arm, slowing their progress.

"What is the matter, Charlotte?"

"My dear Eliza, I meant to tell you that Mr. Darcy is visiting his aunt. I know how much you dislike him."

It embarrassed Elizabeth that she had been so open in expressing her disdain for Mr. Darcy to all who would listen, when they first met. "Oh, Charlotte! My feelings for Mr. Darcy are so decidedly opposed to what they were last autumn."

Charlotte raised her eyebrow in bemusement. Elizabeth smiled sheepishly, grateful for the reprieve from her friend's inquisition as they were shown into the parlour.

When the ladies were introduced to Lady Catherine, she proceeded to introduce Elizabeth to her nephew, Mr. Darcy. Unable to wait a moment longer, Darcy interrupted his aunt by taking Elizabeth's hand and raising it to his lips.

"Miss Elizabeth, I have looked forward to seeing you."

Elizabeth smiled. He did not immediately release her hand, and she did nothing to encourage its freedom.

"The two of you know each other?"

"Yes, your ladyship. Miss Elizabeth and I are acquainted." He remembered to let go.

Elizabeth glanced at Charlotte. She could only imagine the thoughts racing through her clever friend's head, pondering why she no longer disliked the gentleman from Derbyshire, and wondering when the obvious change in sentiments had come about. Thank goodness for Charlotte's sycophantic husband who broke the growing tension in the room by falling all over himself in an attempt to amend for what he deemed his lapse in proper decorum.

Stepping forward, he bowed deeply before his noble patroness. "Forgive me, Lady Catherine, did I fail to mention that my fair cousin and your esteemed nephew, Mr. Darcy, were introduced to each other in Hertfordshire?"

Darcy ignored the man. "My sister is here, as well. She, too, looks forward to seeing you."

At that moment, Georgiana entered the room. She went

straight to Elizabeth. "Miss Elizabeth! My brother said you would be here."

Lady Catherine looked taken aback. With the uneasiness of a stranger in her own home, she said, "You know my niece, as well, young lady?"

"Yes, your ladyship."

Dumbfounded, Lady Catherine stared at her niece. "How can that be? Did you travel to Hertfordshire, too, Georgiana? Why was I not told of this?"

"Miss Elizabeth and I met in town."

"What occasion did you have to meet Miss Elizabeth Bennet in town?"

The entrance of another of Lady Catherine's guests prevented Georgiana's response. Though not as handsome as Mr. Darcy, the older man's address suggested he was very much a gentleman.

"Pray forgive my tardiness, Lady Catherine." He glanced about the room. Every single person save her ladyship and her daughter Anne was still standing.

"Not at all, nephew," Lady Catherine said, exasperated. "It appears Miss Elizabeth Bennet is well acquainted with your cousins. Is she an acquaintance of yours, as well?"

The officer looked at Elizabeth and smiled. "I have not yet had the pleasure. I am Colonel Fitzwilliam, milady. I am honoured to meet you."

"The pleasure is mine, sir."

The remainders of the introductions were made, and the guests took their seats. After some moments, tea was served, and everyone's attention strayed with Lady Catherine's pontificating, speech after speech dictating to the Hunsford guests and her own guests, alike, how they should go about conducting the remainder of their stay.

Elizabeth amused herself by observing the countenance of Charlotte and Mr. Collins as they attended Lady Catherine's every word. Elizabeth could easily surmise where Mr. Darcy might have gleaned his early tutelage on the role of nobility as opposed to those of lesser Society. With such examples as this, how could she fault him? Rosings Park was the epitome of ostentatious wealth with the fine proportions and finished ornaments of its marvellous antechamber, the grand staircases, and magnificent glazing, which by her cousin's account had cost her ladyship's late husband, Sir Lewis de Bourgh, quite a sum.

There sat Lady Catherine, her brownish grey coiffure a-dorning her head in a manner reminiscent of a crown, in all her regal state, as if perched upon a throne. Proclaiming herself a great proficient at music, except for the fact she had never applied herself, the great lady entreated her niece to entertain them on the pianoforte.

Georgiana jumped at the opportunity. "I am happy to exhibit, Lady Catherine. Miss Elizabeth, I should like it if you accompanied me."

"I shall be happy to accompany you. However, I must warn you, my proficiency at the pianoforte leaves much to be desired."

"My brother says otherwise, Miss Elizabeth."

Elizabeth looked at Darcy. He smiled sheepishly. Elizabeth regarded Lady Catherine's pursed lips as disapproval. Nothing good ever came from such a look.

While Georgiana and Elizabeth sat down to decide what they would play, Lady Catherine chastised Darcy and the colonel for her having to spend Easter alone, and she made some mention of this being the first such a time in years.

"I have yet to be given a sufficient reason for the delay." She glared at her youngest nephew. "Do not dare to tell me your delay has anything to do with your stay at Lord Latham's estate, Darcy, for I have since made enquiries, and have learned you took your leave earlier than the rest of the guests."

Elizabeth overheard the entire exchange. Uneasiness crept

over her. What if Lady Catherine had learned even more? Surely, she had not. At least, Elizabeth prayed she had not. She did not know the aristocrat well enough to fathom what she might do with the knowledge of her impropriety, but she suspected her ladyship enough to suppose it would not be good.

"Your information is correct, Lady Catherine. I left Lord Latham's estate earlier than I had planned. However, upon returning to my home, other more pressing matters arose needing my attention."

"Other matters? What was more urgent than honouring your commitment to your family? What business put off your visit by weeks?"

"They were matters of personal nature, your ladyship. I am here now, am I not? I shall speak no more on this subject."

Darcy's strong rebuke served two purposes, at least, for the time being. Lady Catherine was silenced, and Elizabeth's curiosity was spurred.

Throughout their performance, Elizabeth tried to hide her distraction. After two songs, Georgiana brought up the one subject Elizabeth would rather not discuss.

"May I enquire of your youngest sister, Miss Elizabeth? How does she get along?"

Elizabeth wondered what, if anything, Miss Darcy knew of the resolution to the scandalous business.

"I ... my sister is married ... to Mr. Wickham."

"The marriage is a good thing, is it not?" Georgiana diverted her eyes; therefore, Elizabeth was unable to ascertain her feelings on the matter.

"One would hope, Miss Darcy. I suspect you know him well enough to appreciate my scepticism."

"Indeed," the younger woman said. "Miss Elizabeth, I have a confession. I know I promised you that I would say nothing of the unfortunate event. However, I was unable to keep the promise. I told my brother ... thinking he, better than anyone, might be able to help. Please say you forgive me and that you understand my reasoning."

"I understand. After what you had suffered, I believe I was unfair to ask you to shoulder such a weighty burden a-lone."

Elizabeth forced herself to smile. "I know I sound un-happy with the outcome, but in light of what might have oc-curred, I know things turned out for the best. My sister has a chance for respectability. In the end, that is what matters."

The approach of Mr. Darcy and Colonel Fitzwilliam soon ended the ladies' tête-a-tête. Both put on a brave face for the gentlemen's sake and asked for suggestions on what they should play next.

ೞೞೞ

For the third time in as many days, Darcy and Elizabeth walked along a secluded path, enjoying the easiness that had marked their acquaintance since their last meeting in Hert-fordshire. The two talked about the events at Longbourn and wondered how Jane and Bingley fared. Elizabeth hinted of what a difference it would have made had she remained at Longbourn to help her sister along.

"At the risk of sounding crass, I must say I am glad you decided against your pledge to remain at Longbourn as a spin-ster. I believe those were your exact words."

"Perhaps I have not decided against my plan completely. I must not always remain at Longbourn. Besides, I supposed there is little risk of scandal in visiting such a quaint town as this."

"Actually, Lord Latham and I have identified the source of the rumour of our ... our—"

"You might as well say it, Mr. Darcy. The night I spent in your home."

"Yes. Well, it turns out one of his household servants once worked in my home. I believe the situation is well contained. You need not worry on that score any longer."

"I pray no one's livelihood was lost as a result of this incident. Servants will talk."

"True, there is talk, there is gossip, and then there is downright mischief making. In this case, the instigator was a trusted servant who escaped a harsher retribution with a strong reprimand."

"I must confess I am relieved to hear it. I had not put the matter completely out of my mind."

"Trust me, Miss Elizabeth, I am relieved, as well, much more than you know."

"Why is that, sir?"

"Because, the next time I offer you my hand in marriage, I intend to go about it entirely differently."

Some thought of his first proposal could not help crossing her mind. "I am almost afraid to wonder what that might be."

"Allow me to demonstrate, if you will."

Taking her puzzled silence as consent, Darcy took Elizabeth's hand in his. He lowered himself to one knee.

"Miss Elizabeth, you must allow me to tell you how much I love and admire you—"

Thinking he was having a bit of fun, she thought she might as well play along. "I seem to recall hearing those words before, Mr. Darcy. Then again, I may be mistaken."

Darcy hushed her with a finger to her lips. "Miss Elizabeth, because of you, I am bewitched, body and soul. I cannot go on without you. Please do me the honour of accepting my hand."

"Mr. Darcy, please stand up this instant."

"No—not until you give me the answer I long to hear."

"What answer is that, sir?"

"There can only be one answer. Say yes."

"What are you asking? Are you not speaking merely in jest?"

"Miss Elizabeth, from this day forward, I never wish for us to be parted again. I love you. Please, say yes."

She fought her tears. A proposal on bended knee from the man she then knew she loved, the only man she would ever love, for the rest of her days.

"Yes, I will. Nothing would make me happier. I, too, wish never to be parted from you from this day forth."

Darcy stood, wrapped his arms around her in a tight embrace, and lifted her off the ground. After he spun around, he gently placed her on her feet. "You have made me the happiest of men."

He leaned down and gazed into her eyes. "May I?"

Elizabeth silently acquiesced.

Mr. Darcy placed light kisses on her forehead, on her chin, and then, on the tip of her nose. Elizabeth closed her eyes in expectation of what was to come, opening them seconds later in wonderment. He placed a finger atop her parted lips. He leaned down and whispered in her ear. "I have every intention of kissing you properly, my love." He kissed her chin softly. "But not yet."

The two lovers spent the better part of the rest of their time together discussing their joy and planning how their lives as man and wife would be. They parted with an agreement to meet early in the morning in the same spot to determine how they would share the happy news. By Mr. Darcy's account, his aunt would not take the news graciously. They needed a plan.

Chapter 15

Darcy slowed his steed's pace as he approached Elizabeth walking along the lane the next morning. "Fancy seeing you here."

"I rather doubt that, Mr. Darcy. If I know you at all, you have been pacing back and forth anticipating my arrival for some time."

"Indeed, you know me well."

"So, do you intend to remain on your horse or will you join me?"

"I intend to remain here." He extended his hand. "Come ride with me."

Elizabeth looked around. "Do you not think my riding with you is inappropriate?"

"Indeed, entirely inappropriate, scandalous even. If caught, I might even be forced to marry you."

Darcy lifted Elizabeth and sat her side-saddle in front of him. He kissed her upon her forehead. "I am delighted to see you this morning, my love. Why were you late?" He signalled his horse to begin a slow, steady amble along the path.

"I had the unwelcome task of explaining my penchant for long, solitary walks to my cousin, I am afraid. He lectured me on the indelicacy of young, unmarried women wandering about alone at such an early hour."

"I am sorry for being the cause of any discomfort."

"Believe me; I suffer little comfort in the presence of my cousin. Nothing you might do would make the situation worse."

In no time at all, they came to his destination. Crisp white linen, elegant sterling silver candelabras, fine china, polished silverware, and a rich bouquet of fresh spring blossoms a-dorned a table, along with several covered dishes.

Darcy dismounted, handed Elizabeth down, and secured his horse.

"Mr. Darcy, everything is splendid."

Darcy escorted her to her seat and attended her. "I wanted our first meal together as betrotheds to be special. I doubt we shall enjoy another such opportunity once we announce our intentions to our families."

Elizabeth thought for a moment on how things would be once her mother learned of their news. *Bedlam.* "I suppose you are correct. I can hardly believe you went to such trouble."

Darcy took his seat on the opposite side of the table. "I have a confession, my love."

Elizabeth raised her brow. "Oh?"

"Georgiana was instrumental in setting all this up. I can hardly take much credit."

"She knows of our engagement?"

"Yes. I hope that does not disappoint you. She is my closest family, and she is exceedingly fond of you. I could not bear to wait to tell her along with all the others."

"Would you say she is pleased?"

"Yes, I would say that she is ecstatic."

Elizabeth smiled. "I shall look forward to having her as a

sister, especially at Pemberley, with my own sisters so far a-way."

Darcy reached across the table and took her hand. "Your sisters are welcome at Pemberley at any time."

"All of my sisters, Mr. Darcy?"

"All of them."

"You say that now. Pray you shall have no cause for re-gret."

"Never—your family is my family. Forever."

The two shared the rest of the meal in relative quiet. At its completion, he took Elizabeth's hand and led her along a wooded path.

He pulled her into his embrace long enough to put her at ease. He reached down and lifted her chin. She felt her eyes glisten with tears of joy. He kissed her upon her forehead be-fore releasing her. The warmth of his arms aroused familiar-ity—some innate intimacy. She had a sense of having been in his arms before in another time and place. She had not given much thought to their night together in weeks, resolving her lack of recall was a sure sign there was nothing to recall.

What she found too awkward to discuss before seemed natural in light of their current understanding. If perhaps there was more to that night than he had admitted or than she had recollected, surely he would be willing to discuss it now.

"Mr. Darcy, I know you cared for me the evening that I fell ill at your home. What I do not know, sir, is the extent of said care."

"You were quite indisposed for the greater part of the evening, but you must have some recollection of what took place."

"No—I remember nothing at all, save sitting on the set-tee near the fire and later waking in the mistress's suite."

Elizabeth put a bit of space between them. "Do you not think it is time you tell me everything of what happened?"

Darcy closed the distance. "Nothing in comparison to what you should expect on our wedding night, my love. In fact, if you give me leave to serve as your lady's maid on our wedding night, I shall show you everything I did ... as well as everything I did not do, that evening at my home."

"I warn you, sir, I am a selfish creature. Patience is not my strong suit. Besides, have I not waited long enough?"

"Trust me when I say it will be worth the wait. You do trust me, do you not?"

"I trust you."

"Then, let your mind be at ease. Your virtue remains intact." He raised her hand to his lips.

Elizabeth had no choice but to be content with his side-stepping. On another subject, she refused to keep her counsel. Although reluctant to confess his part in the scheme concerning Lydia, in the wake of Elizabeth's overwhelming evidence, he said he, indeed, had a hand in discovering her youngest sister. He had coerced Wickham into marrying her, and paid for his commission in New Castle.

The degradation, the inconvenience, and the expense! The lengths he had taken to ensure a happier outcome than anyone in her family had ever envisioned for Lydia astounded Elizabeth.

"Mr. Darcy, how shall I ever repay your kindness?"

"How can you even ask such a question? Surely, you must know. I did everything for you with no expectation of gratitude. When I told you that I would protect you that day at Lord Latham's, I meant every word of it. I have since considered there is nothing in the world I would not do for you, to protect you and to make certain your happiness."

Darcy raised Elizabeth's hand to his lips and kissed it. He turned her hand over and placed a lingering kiss on the inside of her wrist. "You have made me the happiest man in the world. I can hardly wait for us to be married."

"First, we must share our joyous news with our families."

"Yes. I understand you will be dining at Rosings this evening. We will commence with an announcement before dinner. In a day or two, we shall journey to Hertfordshire to celebrate our happy news with your family."

"Mama will be pleased to know her least favourite daughter is to be married."

"To her least favourite man in the world, no doubt. I clearly recall how Mrs. Bennet barely tolerated my presence when I visited Longbourn."

"I apologise again for Mama's behaviour."

"I am afraid it is I who will be apologising to you before the end of the evening."

"Whatever do you mean?"

"My aunt will not condone our marriage. She will go on and on about my obligations to my family."

"Perhaps Lady Catherine will surprise you. She does not seem nearly as dreadful as I had long supposed."

"Trust me, every semblance of kindness will dissipate once she learns of our engagement. She clings to the hope that Anne and I will marry."

"Yes, of that I am aware. I have long known of your *presumed* engagement on account of Mr. Wickham."

"No doubt." He looked rather disheartened.

Elizabeth linked her arm through Darcy's and silently apologised.

Darcy returned her smile and placed his hand over her hand. "Some mention of George Wickham is inevitable. You need not fret over the matter."

ಬಂಬಂ

Lady Catherine was stunned speechless with the announcement of her favourite nephew's engagement. The calm manner in which she digested the news could best be described as downright eerie. Each one in the room awaited the volcanic eruption that did not come. Perhaps she was merely biding her time. Elizabeth suspected that no one in the room, including herself, knew for sure, and everyone in the room wondered. And worried.

Some evidence of Lady Catherine's acknowledgement of her nephew's happy news surfaced once they had sat down to dinner.

"I suppose, Miss Elizabeth Bennet, your mother and father are pleased with this development."

"We have yet to inform my parents, your ladyship."

"You mean to say they have no knowledge of any of this." Lady Catherine glared at Elizabeth in disbelief. "That is rather strange."

Darcy placed his fork aside. "We have had no time to inform Mr. and Mrs. Bennet. We shall correct that matter when we travel to Hertfordshire in a couple of days."

"A couple of days? Pray you do not intend to compound your earlier slights against me by cutting this visit short. What is the hurry?"

"We are both excited for the Bennets to share in our joy."

"Why travel there when a letter would suffice?"

"I am eager to return home."

"I should imagine you are, but why does my nephew need to take his leave?"

"I have no intention of parting with Miss Elizabeth upon the heels of our engagement." Darcy and Elizabeth's eyes met from across the table. "In fact, we never wish to be parted again."

"Well—I never." Lady Catherine fell silenced. She resumed her earlier stance as regarded the announcement and directed her full attention to her other guests.

When the time came for the ladies to separate from the gentlemen, Darcy suggested that everyone might proceed directly to the drawing room instead.

Lady Catherine looked at him in wild-eyed dismay. "I realise you and Miss Elizabeth Bennet have proclaimed your wishes never to be parted; however, I insist we uphold tradition."

With her pronouncement, the ladies stood to take their leave. Darcy and Elizabeth looked at each other. His eyes reflected his concern. More than anything, she wanted him to see there was no cause for worry.

Lady Catherine hesitated a moment in the hallway, allowing her daughter Anne, Charlotte, Maria, and Georgiana to go on ahead of her.

"Miss Elizabeth Bennet, might I have a moment of your time?"

Elizabeth and Georgiana exchanged questioning glances.

"Now, young woman! Georgiana, run along and join the others."

Georgiana did not look pleased but heeded her aunt's edict. Elizabeth followed her ladyship down the long winding hallway in the opposite direction.

Lady Catherine closed the library door and turned to face Elizabeth.

"You can have no doubt why I have asked for a private audience with you."

"I am afraid I have no idea."

"I will not be trifled with, young lady. I assist upon knowing what you have done to induce my nephew to request your hand in marriage."

"What I have done? Surely, your ladyship knows that the gentleman holds all the power in such instances."

"You must realise I will never stand for this. I offer no excuse for my nephew, except that he has taken leave of his senses. I only have you to blame for that. Were he in his right mind, he would never have proposed such a ridiculous notion. My nephew is engaged to be married to my daughter Anne. What have you to say to that?"

"I know of no such engagement."

"This engagement is of a peculiar kind. The two of them have been promised to each other since their births. I do not intend to allow someone such as you, with such inferior circumstances and such low connections to interrupt my plans. I insist you speak to my nephew and put an end to this nonsense."

"Why would I do such a thing? Mr. Darcy and I have professed our love for each other. He has asked me to marry him, and I have accepted. Nothing you might do or say will influence me otherwise."

"You foolish girl! Do you suppose for one minute that anyone in his family will sanction such an unequal alliance? You will be disdained, derided, and despised, by all who are connected with him. Surely, you do not expect any decent family will receive you. Such an alliance would be a disgrace, an embarrassment to the noble Fitzwilliam family. We shall all turn our backs to you."

"Those are heavy misfortunes. Nevertheless, as Mrs. Darcy, my future happiness is unaffected by such that you have described. I am sure I shall have no cause to repine."

"You mean to say you would allow the man you claim to love to be laughed at, ridiculed, and turned away by everyone he holds dear? Do you not consider that a connection with you must disgrace him in the eyes of everyone of merit? My nephew—brother to the son of his late father's steward? Such a notion is surely unendurable."

Elizabeth flinched. She had not even considered what this must mean to either Mr. Darcy or Miss Darcy. Especially Miss Darcy.

Lady Catherine supposed she had struck a nerve. She determined to carry her point by further haranguing Elizabeth on her scant understanding of what had been the means of recovering Lydia from ruin. Her ladyship's throbbing veins etched across her temple.

"Heaven and earth! What are you thinking? Are the shades of Pemberley to be thus polluted?"

Mr. Darcy opened the library door and stormed into the room. As loud as she was, he no doubt had heard his aunt from all the way down the hall. The sight of the older woman towering over his intended incensed him.

"That is quite enough, Lady Catherine. You have assaulted Miss Elizabeth in the most egregious manner. I insist you apologise this instant, and in no way are you ever to speak to her in this insulting way again if you wish to go on seeing me and enjoying the hospitality of my homes."

"Apologise? I will do no such thing. What I have said to this young lady is nothing compared to what she might expect should the two of you persist in this foolish notion."

"Is this your final resolve? Am I to expect no satisfaction from you as regards atonement for your abuse of my future wife this evening?"

"Never!"

"Then I shall know what to do." Darcy took Elizabeth by the hand. "Come with me, my love. We shall leave this place."

Chapter 16

Jubilation reigned throughout the halls of Longbourn in a perfect uproar! Some version of Elizabeth's happy news had arrived at Longbourn ahead of her, thanks to Mr. Collins. He had sent out an express post-haste the morning after the explosion at Rosings Park, and he conveyed the news in such terms as to cause disparagement on account of the devastation wrought in his noble patroness. Jane sat beside her father at the breakfast table when he read the express, pondering aloud if their poor cousin had suffered a bout of insanity.

Had word of the express rider's arrival not excited the entire household, Mr. Bennet might well have kept the news to himself, preferring to wait until he received an account directly from Elizabeth. Alas, he was bound to share the news with Mrs. Bennet and Jane's other sisters, unleashing a flurry of chatter throughout the halls.

Her mother was beside herself when the stately Darcy carriage arrived. Despite the sudden approbation afforded him by his future mother-in-law, Darcy wasted no time before speaking with Mr. Bennet privately to make it official, leaving Elizabeth and Georgiana to brave the fervent accolades and commendations of the ladies of Longbourn.

Soon thereafter, Jane invited her dearest sister to walk with her. Though the thought of her sister being in love pleased her, suspicion and scepticism could only be abated with an earnest, heartfelt discussion.

"Lizzy, you must tell me everything. I never had any inclination that you were in love with Mr. Darcy. Do you truly love him? How did it happen? When did it happen? Did it happen when you were in town? How could it, for you were not in company with Mr. Darcy whilst in town, or were you? Mr. Bingley mentioned that the three of you were together in Tilbury. Is that when you first—"

"Calm down, dearest Jane, I shall answer all your questions, but I can only answer one at a time."

"Of course, you are correct. Oh! I am so excited for you, Lizzy."

"Your enthusiasm is nothing at all in comparison to my own, I assure you."

"So, how did this all come to be?"

"Jane, as for our being together in town, Mr. Darcy and I crossed paths several times whilst I was in London, so my opinion of him is founded upon a number of things. However, let us discuss first things first. Mr. Darcy and I were guests at the estate of one of his closest friends, Lord Trevor Helmsley, the Earl of Latham. However, we parted under the worst of circumstances.

"I am embarrassed to tell you that Mr. Darcy had proposed marriage to me before, and I had rejected his hand. I confess that the manner of his proposal was such that I was justified in rejecting him despite the fact that his intentions and sentiments were genuine."

"Why ever would you refuse his first offer of marriage?"

Elizabeth hesitated for an instant. No benefit would come from telling her dearest sister what Mr. Darcy had done in separating her from Mr. Bingley. On that point, she kept her counsel. In fact, she had said nothing to Jane of her true purpose in going to town. However, the truth of Wickham's character, now known to all, was safe for discussion.

"You see, Jane, I misjudged him harshly, as you well know. My prejudice towards him was the consequence of his initial slight at the assembly, as much as Mr. Wickham's false accusations against him. Suffice it to say, I threw Mr. Wickham's allegations in his face as sufficient justification for thinking him the most despicable man in the world.

"I imagined myself such a fool upon learning the truth about Mr. Wickham, and not from Mr. Darcy, but rather from Miss Darcy. I, who always had prided myself on my ability to discern other people's true character, had been totally deceived. My shame was great indeed."

"Miss Darcy? What did she have to say?"

"Oh, Jane. Mr. Wickham had taken advantage of her naïvety, much the same as he later did with Lydia. Fortunately, Mr. Darcy saved her in time." Elizabeth went on to tell her sister all that Georgiana had told her.

"I wish Lydia had been as fortunate as Miss Darcy."

"But that is what I am about to tell you. Mr. Darcy also saved Lydia." At length, Elizabeth told the story of how Mr. Darcy had gone about recovering Lydia from the pits of despair, and striking a bargain with Mr. Wickham to marry her.

"I always knew there was a great deal of good in Mr. Darcy. I am happy that you recognise his value, as well, and that you are to be married."

The two sisters embraced. Straightening out, Jane wiped a tear from her face. "I am so happy for you, Lizzy. May I see the ring once more?"

Elizabeth held out her hand for inspection, obliging her sister with a smile as dazzling as the brilliant diamonds in her ring.

"I have never beheld a ring as magnificent."

"Yes, it is so lovely. It belonged to Mr. Darcy's mother, Lady Anne. I shall cherish it, always."

"Just think, one day your own son might bestow this precious heirloom to his betrothed."

Elizabeth's thoughts pirouetted with the prospect of a house full of Darcys. How rich and overflowing with love her life would be with her future husband!

"I always knew you would find such happiness."

"Truly, Jane, I am exceedingly happy. Now I only need to learn how things are progressing with you and Mr. Bingley. Tell me that you two are well on your way to establishing an understanding so that my happiness shall be complete."

Her eyes failing to contain her tears, Jane smiled. "Dear Lizzy, I will only say that our father should expect a visit from two handsome gentlemen today."

ဆလဆလ

She entered the library, upon hearing from her betrothed of her father's wish to speak with her, in time to see him pacing the floor, his countenance somewhat befuddled. "Lizzy, are you quite certain Mr. Darcy is the man for you? When last he was here, one would have sworn you hated the man."

"No, Papa. I do not hate him. I love him. I love Mr. Darcy."

"How did this happen?"

"Papa, my tender regard for Mr. Darcy has been coming on for some time. I hardly know when it began, but I am sure that once I had made a start, it was all I could do not to think of him. He means everything to me. He is the best man I know. He is selfless and generous, and there is nothing on earth he would not do for those whom he loves."

"Generous, you say? Has this anything to do with his fortune? Yes, Mr. Darcy is as generous as any man of his means has the luxury of being, should he wish it. You shall be rich beyond anyone's dreams, but will that make you happy?"

"I am exceedingly happy. Wait until I tell you what he has done—" Elizabeth gave her father a full account of everything that Mr. Darcy had taken upon himself on behalf of their family.

In the middle of her recount, Mr. Bennet sat down, stood up, and sat back down again whilst registering it all. He was amazed that someone so wholly unconnected to his family would go to such measures. He spoke enthusiastically of his relief as he realised his brother-in-law had not shouldered the burden. This way, Mr. Bennet might dismiss the notion that, theretofore, weighed heavily upon his mind—that he would have to repay Mr. Gardiner. Surely, a man as wealthy as his future son-in-law would be in no need of restitution.

After some discussion on the timing of the joyous occasion, Mr. Bennet sent his favourite daughter on her way with his blessings, a happy man indeed. By the glimmer in his eyes, his happiness increased twofold when Elizabeth opened the door of the library to find Mr. Bingley standing there, his hand poised mid-air in readiness to knock.

"Mr. Bingley, come inside. I have been expecting this visit for some time."

છાશ૦ઈ

Darcy had left Mr. Bennet's library a happier man, even if a bit confounded, than when he had entered. He avoided the company of his future mother and sisters-in-law by waiting outside of the door for Elizabeth to emerge from her father's library. As pleased as he had been to see that his friend had also decided to seek a private audience with Mr. Bennet, he could not help but bestow his good wishes absent-mindedly. He had matters of far greater importance on his mind, namely, how long it would be before he and Elizabeth became man and wife. Did Mr. Bennet honestly expect him to wait three months? Darcy could not wait to speak with Elizabeth in private.

"Is there somewhere we might talk? After my interview with your father, I am dying to have you all to myself."

"Shall we walk to the pond? If we leave through the back, no one should notice we have disappeared."

"Yes, please, lead the way."

Elizabeth looked around mischievously and then took him by the hand and led him outside. Once they were settled in a comfortable spot along the water's edge, he raised her hand and brushed his lips over her fingertips. He then studied the ring he had slipped on her finger the day before and marvelled at his good fortune in having won the heart of the woman of his dreams.

"You have not uttered a word since we left the house. Is there something amiss, Mr. Darcy?

"Forgive me, my love."

"Did Papa say anything to upset you?"

"Why? What did he say to you?"

"He gave me his blessing, of course."

"Elizabeth, I realise your father is known for his dry humour. I pray that is the case now. He suggested we might wait three months before marrying."

"A three-month courtship sounds delightful. Mama will be overjoyed."

Darcy was not impressed. He said nothing, but his countenance betrayed his disappointment. His desire for her wreaked havoc on his mind and his body, but he was determined their relationship would remain chaste—no more than light kisses until their wedding night.

Three months?

Even Elizabeth thought a courtship of three months was absurd. She had told her father as much. She thought, however, she might have a bit of fun with Mr. Darcy. Alas, his look of dismay told her that he had not yet learned to laugh at himself, and she thought perhaps now was not the time to teach him. They had a lifetime for that.

She then raised his hand to her mouth and brushed his knuckles against her lips. "Why such a forlorn look, dearest?"

"Again, I must beg your forgiveness, my love. I am a selfish man, and I have been used to having my way. I am endeavouring to change in that regard, and whilst I do not wish to wait that long, I will if needs be."

"You must not be too hard upon yourself. Besides, I am equally as selfish in that regard. I long for nothing more than to be your wife. Papa is quite aware of my sentiments, so you need not fret." Smiling, she fought to restrain the giggle that threatened to bubble forth.

"You are laughing at me."

"I am guilty as charged." Unable to repress her laughter a second longer, the sound of it brought a smile to his face. "Do you forgive me?"

"Of course—you need not ask, for I would forgive you anything."

"And you have proven as much, sir." Her countenance quickly turned sober. "I am embarrassed even now when I think of how badly I abused you in the past with my unguarded tongue."

"What did you ever say to me that I did not deserve? You accused me of being haughty and disdainful towards those I considered beneath me. With few exceptions, my actions proved your words as truth. I offered you my hand in marriage with every expectation that you would accept me, and that you would be grateful. Watching you walk away from me at Latham Hall was a painful revelation. I knew that were I to win your heart, I needed to think of others ahead of my own interests. I learned that all my wealth and fortune meant nothing if I could not prove myself to be a man worthy of your respect."

Elizabeth touched his chin. "You are worthy of my respect and so much more. I love you, Mr. Darcy."

"It warms my heart to hear that, at long last, for I have been in love with you for as long as I can recall."

"Yes, and it pleases me immensely to hear you say it. Still, I am curious to know when did you first realise you love me?" Elizabeth smiled impishly. "Surely, you did not love me that afternoon when I arrived on your doorstep."

"I am rather certain I was in love with you, even then."

"Well, I have to say you did an excellent job of hiding that fact from me."

Darcy pulled Elizabeth into the cradle of his embrace. She rested her back against his broad chest, as he brushed her hair aside and feathered light kisses along her neckline. "Did I?"

His actions silenced her as her mind drifted to that rainy day in his home and the way he had looked at her. His looks then were as smouldering as his looks of late. Her heart raced.

If this is an indication of how I will feel as his betrothed, I know not how I might survive even weeks of waiting, much less months, to become Mrs. Darcy.

"Mr. Darcy, now that I recall, I believe I heard Mama mention a special licence."

Having relinquished the comfort of his arms and repositioned herself to see his face, she observed the astounding effect that her words wrought on his handsome countenance.

"A special licence, you say?" He kissed her cheek. "Indeed."

Chapter 17

Lord Latham was not surprised to hear of Darcy's impending marriage to Miss Elizabeth Bennet; neither was Lady Gwendolen, for that matter. Darcy had told his friend of his earlier failure to win Elizabeth's hand, even discussing the ungentlemanly manner in which he had gone about his proposal. Having accepted his friend's resolve to make amends to the woman he loved, Lord Latham sat his sister down and told her the future she had long wished for with Darcy would never be.

Both brother and sister had decisions to make, and hence they did. Lord Latham, in seeing the joy Elizabeth brought to his friend's life, decided he wanted such a life for himself. He determined the life that he wanted to lead was not the life his ladylove wished for, and thus he must let her go, affording both of them chances for true happiness.

Lady Gwendolen concluded she would embrace Mr. Darcy's happiness. He was her brother's best friend; therefore, their future paths would always cross. She had promised her brother she would never repeat a word of the rumour about Mr. Darcy and Miss Elizabeth. She remained true to her word. She reckoned she had been nothing but honest by enlightening Miss Elizabeth of Mr. Darcy's hand in separating her sister from Mr. Bingley. Miss Elizabeth had forgiven him; surely, she bore no grudge against her, a mere messenger.

Lady Catherine clung to her vitriol with a vengeance until she learned, by way of a conversation with Charlotte, of a connection between the future Mrs. Darcy and Lady Susan Townes. Indeed, it was the same Lady Townes who was connected to Lord and Lady Langley, and thus Lord Latham and his sister Lady Gwendolen Helmsley. Lady Catherine was intrigued by her discovery. Such advantageous connections as these gave her quite a bit to work with. Yes, perhaps she might make something of Miss Elizabeth Bennet from Longbourn and Hertfordshire after all.

Caroline Bingley received the news of her brother's engagement with vexation. All her efforts to promote an alliance between Miss Darcy and her brother, not to mention Mr. Darcy and herself, had been in vain. She had lost on both counts to two daughters of a common country gentleman. Nevertheless, Caroline was clever. She did not intend to lose her place amongst Society, afforded to her by her brother and his friend, Mr. Darcy. She wrote warm letters of commendations and praise to both Elizabeth and Jane as a means of assuring she would always enjoy a seat at the dinner tables at Pemberley and Netherfield Park.

Though happy, Lady Susan was not as pleased as she might have been with the news. She had grown rather fond of Sir Robert Boxley. She wanted nothing more than to see him well settled with a respectable young lady such as Miss Elizabeth Bennet. Then again, she had some measure of hope. She rather enjoyed the role of matchmaker. It suited her and gave her purpose.

Mrs. Gardiner received the news of her favourite niece's engagement with a sense of accomplishment. She recalled how Elizabeth had been forced to spend the night at Darcy House and remembered thinking at the time that her niece protested a bit too much as regarded her sentiments towards the gentleman from Pemberley and Derbyshire. Crediting herself with the thought that in inviting her niece to spend the Season in town, and putting her in the path of gentlemen of Mr. Darcy's standing by way of Lady Susan, she supposed she had been the means of uniting them.

Georgiana's fondest wish had long been that her brother would marry Miss Elizabeth Bennet ever since the moment of their introduction, or lack thereof, when she saw her asleep in the mistress's suite at Darcy House. Happy indeed was she to gain not one, but five sisters. Georgiana, Mary, and Kitty became fast friends, which pleased Mrs. Bennet exceedingly. One daughter settled, two daughters engaged, with the last two destined to be thrown into the paths of many rich men. Mrs. Bennet thanked God for her ample blessings. Her work was done.

รรร

The soft patter of rain against the windows in her new room brought to mind an earlier time. Illuminated by the fire's warm glow, the room was already familiar to her, replete with its mystery, as well as its promise.

A light rap on the adjoining door interrupted her musings. Her husband pushed it open slowly, pausing at the doorway out of respect to her modesty.

"May I join you, Mrs. Darcy?"

She stood to receive him. "I have been waiting for you." Nervousness, excitement—Elizabeth embodied all this and more. She loved this man. Darcy stepped inside, closed the distance between them with long strides, and took her hand in his. Raising it to his lips, he kissed it.

"Are we alone for the rest of the night?"

"Indeed. I believe you offered to serve as my lady's maid this evening."

"Yes, I promised to demonstrate for you everything that occurred during your first night here. You did not forget." Darcy took both her hands in his, favouring each of her palms with soft kisses.

"I have managed to think of little else."

He ceased his tender ministrations and gazed into her dark, bewitching eyes. *Beyond compare.* "Then, you shall wait no longer."

Elizabeth's fluttering stomach danced in tune with her heart's racing beat.

Darcy placed his hand against her face. "First, I wish to start by saying that on your first night ever in this room, I did not do this." Elizabeth closed her eyes in anticipation. Would this be the moment? He had kept her waiting, wishing, longing for that moment through weeks of courtship. His soft lips met hers, tentatively at first, before engulfing them in deliverance of the promise of something wonderful.

Eyes still closed, Elizabeth caught her breath. "You did not?" An inkling of what she had been missing sparked a bit of yearning.

"No." The caress of his soft whisper against her ear promised more.

"What did you do?"

"Allow me to start at the beginning. I returned to my study, prepared to serve you the tea I had laboured over in the kitchen, and I was alarmed. I did not see you. I thought you had braved the rain and tried to return home on your own.

"Then, I noticed you on the settee, sound asleep."

"Did you even attempt to awaken me?"

"I knelt beside you and spoke your name. At first, I worried when you did not heed my pleas to awaken, and then you did respond. You sat up, stating your desire to change out of your wet things. I was about to show you into another room for privacy, but upon standing, you collapsed.

Elizabeth gasped aloud. Darcy quieted her with a finger to her lips. "I captured you in my arms and carried you to my room."

As he re-enacted the events of that evening by picking her up and carrying her into the adjoining suite, Elizabeth's mouth gaped open, forming an enticing, perfect circle.

"What? This was the only upstairs apartment with a warm fire."

Elizabeth held her feigned protest. Darcy placed her gently on his bed. "My only thought was to keep you as warm as possible until I prepared a fire in the adjoining room.

"You never once stirred. I left you here whilst I prepared the fire, and afterward, I ventured to my sister's room to select one of her nightgowns."

"Your sister's nightgown?"

"I could not leave you in your own clothing."

"Please continue, Mr. Darcy."

"I will not demonstrate my next step. Suffice it to say, I returned to this room, found you still asleep, picked you up and carried you off to bed."

The gentle pressure of his hard body against hers as he sat on the bed quelled her anxiety over what might have happened in the past and increased her longing for what was to come.

"One by one, I unfastened your dress, like so." He fingered the tiny hooks. "Now here is where I beg your permission to commence showing what I did not do. As I recall, the gown you wore at the time did not have nearly as many buttons as this one, and I most certainly did not do this."

He paused between each catch and traced kisses along her neckline. Waves of nervous tremors flooded her body with each brush of his lips.

Darcy ceased speaking as he lowered her gown from her shoulder. He was as pleased in that instant as he was the first time with the discovery of the simplicity of her corset. Elizabeth's slender figure did not lend itself to heavy bindings and the like. He slowly unlaced the strings. All thoughts of how he had managed such an intimate undertaking gave way to the splendour of the soft touch of his lips against her shoulders. Elizabeth collapsed against the cradle of his embrace, granting unfettered access to the length of her neckline. He lowered the rest of her undergarments from her shoulders, reached for the silken nightgown he had chosen and even laid out, and slipped it over her head.

"There, everything was done easily and rather properly, all things considered." After demonstrating how he lowered the nightgown over her garments, he made fast work of removing her remaining clothing."

"There you have it, my love. From here, I pulled back the covers and tucked you into bed."

Breathless with desire, Elizabeth smiled. "So, I was right not to have worried these past months that either of us had crossed any boundaries when I stayed here."

"Indeed. Now, let me show you all the rest that I did not do our first night alone."

Her husband slowly proceeded, discarding any and everything hindering his purposes for the evening, and he commenced showing her and teaching her all that he would do every night for the rest of their lives together as man and wife—cherishing, loving, and worshiping her reverently, body and soul.

The Author

P O Dixon writes Jane Austen *Pride and Prejudice* adaptations with one overriding purpose in mind—falling in love with Darcy and Elizabeth. Sometimes provocative, always entertaining, her stories are read, commented on, and thoroughly enjoyed by thousands of readers worldwide.

Connect with P O Dixon Online

Blog: http://podixon.blogspot.com

Twitter: @podixon

Facebook: http://www.facebook.com/podixon

Pinterest: http://pinterest.com/podixon

Website: http://podixon.com

Email: podixon@podixon.com

Other **P O Dixon** *Pride and Prejudice* Variations

He Taught Me to Hope

Darcy and the Young Knight's Quest

"Fitzwilliam Darcy has been many things, angel, werewolf, rock star, and cowboy, but King Arthur? Yes! King Arthur! P.O. Dixon's *He Taught Me To Hope* is a new spin on a most beloved story. And it works!"

"The plot had just the right pacing and the perfect balance of humor, tension, and hot, but chaste, passion to keep the reader captivated." **Leatherbound Reviews**

The Mission

He Taught Me to Hope Christmas Vignette

If you enjoyed **He Taught Me to Hope: Darcy and the Young Knight's Quest** and you find yourself longing to catch up with the Darcys, why not share Ben's first Christmas at Pemberley?

The precocious young lad has invited everyone. Find out what he's up to!

Still a Young Man

Darcy Is In Love

Highlights

Refusing to suffer anyone's pity, the heroine hides the unpleasant truth of her forced marriage from everyone.

Having observed the mourning period for a deceased husband she did not love, she looks forward to enjoying a Season in town.

Her liveliness, her beauty, and her charms attract the notice of unscrupulous people posing as friends.

There's only one man able to help her navigate the treacherous waters of the ton.

To Have His Cake (and Eat It Too)

Mr. Darcy's Tale

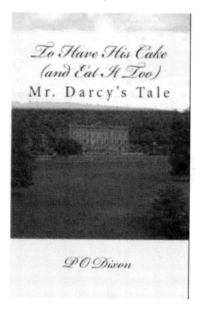

Fitzwilliam Darcy had the best of intentions towards Miss Elizabeth Bennet.

His sense of duty to his family prohibited him from offering her marriage.

His love for her prohibited him from attempting to make her his mistress.

What then, is a man of means supposed to do when he realizes he cannot live without the only woman he will ever love?

** Thousands of copies sold **

What He Would Not Do

Mr. Darcy's Tale Continues

If you enjoyed *To Have His Cake (and Eat It Too),* read this book too.

Having overcome the many seeming obstacles to marrying Miss Elizabeth Bennet, his former employee and the woman of his dreams, Fitzwilliam Darcy must now reaffirm his promise to be a man truly worthy of her affections.

Confronted with the intimate knowledge of her husband's rakish past, Elizabeth too is obliged to reconsider long held tenets that otherwise threaten to tear them apart.

Find out what a newly married Mr. Darcy would not do for family, for friendship, for honor, for love.

1469558R00105

Made in the USA
San Bernardino, CA
19 December 2012